USBORNE UNDERSTANDING SCIENCE
ASTRONOMY

Stuart Atkinson

Edited by
Cheryl Evans

Designed by
Stephen Wright

Illustrated by
Gary Bines

Additional designs by
John Russell

Star charts illustrated by
Blue Chip illustration

Expert checker: **Brian Jones**

Special thanks to Frank Andrews, Carter
Observatory, Wellington, NZ

Contents

In 1986 the European Space Agency probe Giotto took the first ever close-up photographs of a comet - Halley's.

The huge planet Jupiter has 16 moons. These are some of them.

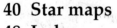
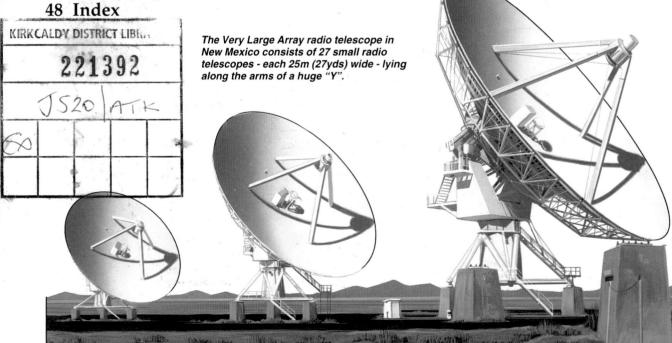

The Very Large Array radio telescope in New Mexico consists of 27 small radio telescopes - each 25m (27yds) wide - lying along the arms of a huge "Y".

The night sky

Most people have looked up at the starry sky on clear nights and wondered how anyone ever made sense of it and gave names to all of its points of light. You may think you need a telescope to study the heavens. However, if you take a little time and really look at the night sky you will be amazed at just how much you can see with your naked eye. You can see the Moon, five planets and thousands of stars. Once you have more experience you will be able to find fainter and more exotic objects like clusters of stars, comets, asteroids and distant galaxies too. You will find out about all of these later on.

About stars

Stars are globes of very hot gas many times larger than Earth. Depending on how hot they are, they may shine blue, yellow or red.

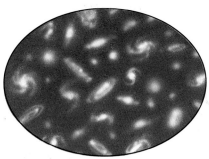

Stars are so far away that you can only see them as points of light. They are grouped together in huge masses of many millions called galaxies.

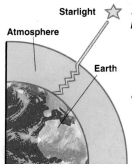

Starlight

Atmosphere

Earth

As a star's light passes through Earth's shifting atmosphere it is distorted and broken up. The stars then appear to flash. This is what makes stars "twinkle".

Stars come in all different sizes. Some are much bigger than others; and although they all appear to be the same distance away from us in the night sky, they are not. You can only tell how far away or big a star is by complex calculations.

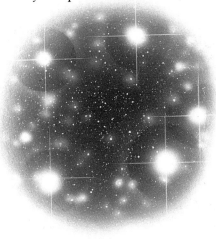

When you look up you are really looking out from Earth into deep space, upon an endless ocean of stars.

The stars scattered across the night sky can be joined up to make patterns called "asterisms". They are parts of larger, well-defined groups of stars called "constellations". These are named after animals, people and objects but very few look anything like the thing they're supposed to be.

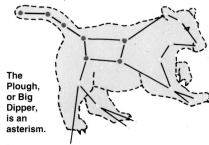

The Plough, or Big Dipper, is an asterism.

It is part of the constellation called Ursa Major, or The Great Bear.

In fact, the night sky is divided up into 88 constellations. You need to learn them if you are to find faint, exotic objects as they can guide you to them like a map of the sky.

The Moon

The Moon is very easy for budding astronomers to observe. It is very big and bright, and you can watch it change its shape from a thin crescent to a full disc.

Some people say the dark patches on the Moon look like a face. See what they really are on page 13.

How to spot a planet

Planets are very different to stars. Planets go around, or orbit, stars like runners around an oval track. Unlike stars, planets don't shine with their own light, but they reflect the Sun's light like mirrors, so they do shine brightly and are often confused with stars. The planets' slow movement through the night sky as they orbit the Sun gives them away.

Stars radiate light like this.

Planets reflect light from their disc.

Stars are so far away they look like points of light in the night sky. Planets are smaller, but much closer to us, so you can see them as tiny discs.

Observing the night sky

To see the night sky at its best you have to go to a place well away from the artificial lights of towns and cities, such as the countryside or a park. Always ask permission if you are planning a trip like this, and go with an adult. After a while you will find that you can see many more stars than you ever have before, as your pupils open wider to let more light into your eye. This process is called "dark adaption".

The Solar System

Many objects of different shapes and sizes go around, or orbit, the Sun. There are thousands of large, irregularly-shaped chunks of metal and rock called asteroids; huge amounts of dust scattered in all directions; large, dirty masses of ice called comets and at least nine planets. Together, this collection of objects is known as The Solar System. Solar means "of the Sun".

Moons

Many of the planets in our Solar System have small companions going around them, called moons or satellites. Earth has only one but Saturn has 18. One of Saturn's moons, Titan, is bigger than the planet Mercury.

Earth's moon

What is gravity?

Gravity is an invisible power called a force, which attracts, or pulls things together. It exists between every object in the Solar System and beyond. The planets and all the other members of the Solar System are held in their orbits by the Sun's powerful gravity.

This picture shows the main objects in the Solar System. It cannot show realistically how far apart they are, as the distances are so vast. You can see their sizes relative to each other at the top of the page opposite.

What are the planets like?

Several different types of planets orbit the Sun. Those closest to it are small, rocky and very compact. The ones further away are mostly larger and made of gas, ice and liquids.

How did the Solar System form?

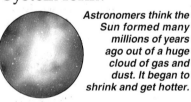

Astronomers think the Sun formed many millions of years ago out of a huge cloud of gas and dust. It began to shrink and get hotter.

As gravity (see above) pulled more and more gas and dust into the cloud, the pressure in the middle increased dramatically.

The high temperature and pressure triggered violent nuclear reactions (see page 6), and a brilliant ball of fire was born - our Sun.

The material left over eventually formed into the many planets, comets and asteroids which orbit the Sun.

1

2

3

4

5

Neptune   Uranus

Pluto

Earth   Mercury

Mars   Venus

**This shows how big the planets
are compared to each other.**

Saturn   Jupiter   The Sun

Mercury, Venus, Earth and Mars
are known as the Inner
Planets. The rest
are the Outer
Planets.

Where does the Solar System end?

Astronomers think that the Solar System
probably extends far beyond Pluto. Recently,
they have found some evidence of this idea in
the form of small "mini-planets" beyond Pluto.
Karla is a 320km (200mi) chunk of red ice which
is between 38 and 56 times further from the Sun
than Earth. Some experts think the
Solar System's boundary could
be marked by a huge halo of
comets called the "Oort
Cloud", named after the
Dutch astronomer Jan
Oort, who suggested its
existence.

*The Oort Cloud may surround the
Sun and its family like a round cage.*

The only one?

Until a few years ago there was no real evidence
to suggest there were planets in orbit around any
star except our Sun. Now, ground-based
telescopes and orbiting observatories have shown
that several other stars at least have discs of
matter swirling around them, which may be in the
process of forming planets; but even if some of the
nearest stars have fully-formed planets in orbit
around them, our current instruments are just not
good enough to see them against the stars' glare.

Key

1. Icy Pluto is usually furthest
from the Sun.
2. Neptune is a turquoise-blue
ball of gases.
3. Uranus rolls around the Sun
on its side.
4. Jupiter is the largest planet.
5. Earth is the only planet
known to have life on it.
6. Saturn has a beautiful
system of icy rings.
7. Mars is cold and dusty and
only half the size of Earth.
8. Asteroids are chunks of
rock and metals. Most lie in a
belt between Mars and Jupiter.
9. Venus is the same size as
Earth.
10. Mercury is the closest
planet to the Sun.
11. Comets are like huge
icebergs which orbit the Sun.

The Sun

The Sun is the most familiar astronomical object of all: it's a blindingly-bright, yellow-white disc in the daytime sky which hides everything else in Space from view. It provides heat and light until it sets and only then the sky becomes dark enough for us to see the stars.

What is the Sun?

The Sun is a massive ball of glowing gas. Inside, atoms of hydrogen are continually split apart and their fragments brought together - or fused - in a different structure to form helium. This is called a Nuclear Fusion Reaction. It produces huge amounts of energy.

The Nuclear Fusion Reaction is a cycle:

A nucleus is the middle part of an atom. A proton is part of a nucleus.

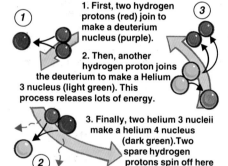

1. First, two hydrogen protons (red) join to make a deuterium nucleus (purple).

2. Then, another hydrogen proton joins the deuterium to make a Helium 3 nucleus (light green). This process releases lots of energy.

3. Finally, two helium 3 nucleii make a helium 4 nucleus (dark green). Two spare hydrogen protons spin off here and start again.

Energy

In fact, the Sun is a star. All the stars you can see in the night sky are also huge balls of glowing gas, but they are so far away they look just like points of light.

Astronomical Units

The planets do not stay exactly the same distance from the Sun all the time, because their orbits are ellipses (oval shapes), not perfect circles. The difference between Earth's nearest and farthest points from the Sun is 5 million km (3.1 million mi). The Earth's average distance from the Sun is 149,600,000km (92,977,000mi). This distance is also known as one Astronomical Unit (AU).

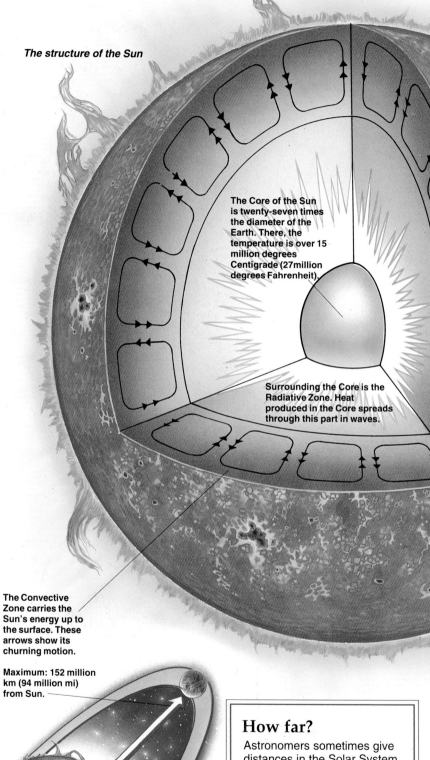

The structure of the Sun

The Core of the Sun is twenty-seven times the diameter of the Earth. There, the temperature is over 15 million degrees Centigrade (27million degrees Fahrenheit).

Surrounding the Core is the Radiative Zone. Heat produced in the Core spreads through this part in waves.

The Convective Zone carries the Sun's energy up to the surface. These arrows show its churning motion.

Maximum: 152 million km (94 million mi) from Sun.

Minimum: 147 million km (91 million mi) from Sun.

How far?

Astronomers sometimes give distances in the Solar System as AUs. Can you say how many AUs it is from the Sun to Neptune, if it is 4,496 million km (2,794 million mi)? Answer on page 35.

Features on the Sun

The corona is made of very thin gas shaped by the Sun's magnetism. It extends for a vast distance, but is very faint and cannot be seen unless the Sun's disc is blocked out, for instance by an eclipse (see right).

The Sun's surface looks as if it is marked with small, dark patches. These are called sunspots and they are areas of the surface which are slightly cooler than their surroundings.

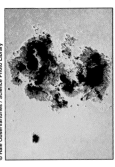

Sometimes sunspots form in groups which can grow enormous. Very large groups may even be visible to the naked eye. The largest group yet seen covered an area of 18,130 million square km (7,000 million square mi).

Sunspots may be surrounded by bright patches called faculae. They are clouds of glowing gas which hover just above the Sun's surface. Much larger clouds of gas, called prominences, explode up from the surface, too. They may look like feathery red arches, streamers or columns of fire reaching up into Space. Even more violent are solar flares.

The Photosphere is the Sun's "surface". It is made out of churning gases and is not solid.

Solar flares are huge explosions which often occur above sunspots and send large amounts of radiation out into space.

Total solar eclipse

A total solar eclipse is when the Moon passes in front of the Sun, covering its face and blocking its light. The Moon can cover the Sun because although it is much smaller, it is also much closer to us. Close one eye and hold up a coin between your face and a ceiling light to see how it works.

The Moon slides over the face of the Sun.

The Sun is totally eclipsed and its corona can be seen.

During a total solar eclipse the corona is seen clearly as a beautiful, blue-white halo around the Sun. Prominences can appear as crimson tongues of flame around the disc's edge.

Auroras

When the radiation that is produced by solar flares reaches Earth it can cause beautiful displays of moving light in the sky, which are best seen from near the Earth's poles. These Northern and Southern Lights resemble slowly-moving curtains, streamers and beams of red, green and blue light. Sometimes they can be so bright that they cast shadows.

Looking safely at the Sun

Astronomers use special methods to study the Sun. However, there is a safe way for you to observe it, too. Simply point a pair of binoculars up at the Sun with a piece of white cardboard behind them. DO NOT LOOK THROUGH THE LENSES AND NEVER LOOK DIRECTLY AT THE SUN. IT CAN BLIND YOU. Move the binoculars around until a bright circle appears. Then focus them until the Sun's image is sharp.

Sun's image
Sunspots show as tiny dark spots.
Cover one lens.
Sun's light enters lens.

Mercury

The closest planet to the Sun is tiny Mercury. In astronomical terms, it orbits very close to the Sun: its average distance is just 57.9 million km (36 million mi).

When to see Mercury

Because it orbits so close to the Sun, Mercury always appears close to it in the sky. That means it can only be seen just before sunrise or after sunset, when the brilliant Sun is beneath the horizon. To the naked eye Mercury looks like a bright star close to the horizon. Through a telescope, Mercury changes shape. It grows from a slim crescent to an almost full disc, like a miniature version of our Moon. Astronomers call these shapes phases.

Days and years

The length of a planet's day and its year depend on how far it is from the Sun, and how quickly it spins around. A planet's year is how many Earth days it takes to travel once all the way around the Sun. A planet's day is how long it takes to rotate once.

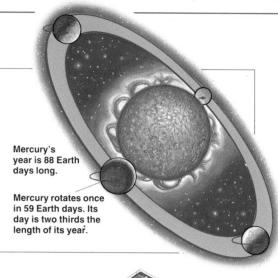

Mercury's year is 88 Earth days long.

Mercury rotates once in 59 Earth days. Its day is two thirds the length of its year.

Ice on Mercury

Being so close to the Sun, daytime temperatures on Mercury can reach 427°C (800°F); but when the Sun is below the horizon the temperature can fall to as low as -183°C (-300°F). Some experts think that despite being so close to the Sun, Mercury may still have ice on its surface. It may be hidden in the shadows at the bottom of very deep craters which lie at its poles. They are so deep that sunlight may never have reached their bases.

The Sun's rays are not at a steep enough angle to reach the depths of the craters.

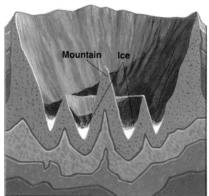

Mountain   Ice

The only spaceprobe to visit Mercury so far is the United States' Mariner 10. It was launched in November 1973 and took many photographs.

The surface of Mercury

Although no markings can be seen clearly on its surface from Earth with a telescope, Mercury was mapped in great detail by the Mariner 10 spaceprobe. The probe discovered that Mercury is a dead world, with no atmosphere and no water. Its rocky surface is entirely covered in sharp-edged craters.

The largest feature seen so far on Mercury is the Caloris Basin, a vast plain 1,300km (808mi) wide, ringed by mountains up to 2km (over 1 mile) high.

The craters on Mercury are smoother and less deep than those on our Moon.

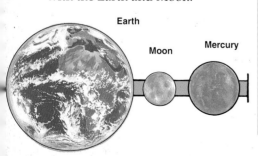

The bright spot in the middle of the photograph is Mercury.

How big is Mercury?

Mercury is a very small planet. In fact, its diameter of 4,878km (3,032mi) makes it the second smallest planet in the Solar System. Here you can see it shown in scale with the Earth and Moon.

Earth

Moon   Mercury

Birthday puzzle

If you arrived on Mercury just in time for your 10th birthday party and stayed there for nine Mercurian years, how old would you be, in Earth years, at the end of your stay? Answer on page 35.

The metal planet

Mercury is so interesting to astronomers because of its interior. The space probe Mariner 10's instruments allowed us to study what lay beneath the surface. They found that it has only a thin crust covering a much thicker metal core, like a ball bearing covered by a thin shell of rock. Almost 70% of Mercury's mass (its size and weight) lies in its huge metal core. It has a diameter of 3,600km (2,237mi). Earth, Venus and Mars, on the other hand, have small cores and thick crusts.

Surface

Crust

Core

Why is Mercury so different?

One theory is that many millions of years ago, Mercury was hit twice by objects almost as large as itself. The first impact almost melted it and all its heavy material sank, making the large core. The second impact ripped away most of the crust.

Metallic core forming.

Thin crust only left.

On Mercury, the Sun would look larger and brighter than it appears in Earth's sky.

Mountains

Craters

If you landed on Mercury you might see a desolate scene like this.

Here, Mariner 10 is flying high above Mercury's barren surface.

Lobate scarps are ranges of incredibly high cliffs, up to 500km (300mi) long. They may have formed when Mercury's core cooled and its brittle crust buckled and wrinkled as the planet shrank.

Magnetic surprise

Mariner 10 found that Mercury has a very weak magnetic field, one hundredth as strong as Earth's. Astronomers thought Mercury's slow rotation and solid core meant it should not have one. They now think that the outside of the core is just molten enough to move and create a magnetic field.

To have a magnetic field, scientists think a planet must have movement in its molten core.

Venus

Venus is the second planet from the Sun and orbits it at an average distance of 108 million km (67 million mi). It can be seen easily with just the naked eye at certain times of the year, just before sunrise or after sunset. Many people call it the Morning or the Evening Star. When its orbit brings Venus closest to Earth, it is the brightest thing in the sky after the Sun and Moon and can even cast shadows.

Venus's atmosphere

Not even the most powerful telescopes on Earth can see any features on the surface of Venus. This is because its surface is hidden from view beneath a very thick atmosphere. It consists mainly of carbon dioxide gas and is so dense that it presses down on the surface like a great weight. People will probably never set foot on Venus, because they would be choked by the unbreathable air, crushed by the enormous pressure and burned by the sulphuric acid which rains from the sky.

Venus's atmosphere is also responsible for the planet's brightness. The clouds act like a huge mirror, reflecting the Sun's blazing light back into space.

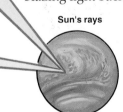

Sun's rays

Most of the Sun's light cannot penetrate Venus's thick atmosphere, but bounces off it.

Earth's beautiful twin

Because it shone so beautifully in the night sky, the Ancient Romans named Venus after their Goddess of Love. Because Venus is almost the same size as Earth, astronomers in the past wondered if it might be Earth's twin, but with an even greater variety of life because it was warmer.

Hot-house

Although it is further from the Sun than Mercury, Venus is hotter because heat which does get through the clouds is trapped, making the temperature rise, as in a greenhouse. This is why it is called the Greenhouse Effect. Scientists are worried that man-made gases which are rising into Earth's atmosphere may trap heat and cause the same effect here.

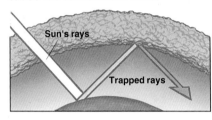

Sun's rays

Trapped rays

Venus revealed

Venus kept its secrets until the Space Age. In 1975 its surface was photographed by two Soviet Venera probes. They found it was covered in sharp-edged rocks and looked like a gloomy, orange-brown desert. Venus's atmosphere prevented early probes from photographing the surface from orbit, so later ones used radar to peer through the clouds. Their maps showed Venus was mostly flat with several large continents.

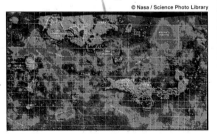

© Nasa / Science Photo Library

Ishtar Terra, at the top, is as big as Australia and is dominated by the towering Maxwell Montes mountains. Aphrodite Terra is as large as Africa, and looks like a scorpion with a curved tail.

Strange days

Venus rotates very slowly. In fact, it takes longer to rotate once (243 days) than it does to orbit the Sun (224 days), so its day is actually longer than its year.

Retrograde rotation

Earth and most other planets spin this way.

Only Venus spins the other way.

Venus doesn't just spin slowly, it also spins in the opposite direction to the Earth and most other planets. This is called retrograde rotation. It means that if you were standing on Venus the Sun would rise in the West and set in the East.

Observing Venus

Like Mercury, Venus shows phases. Some people can see its crescent with their naked eye, but if your eyesight isn't that good you can see Venus's phases with binoculars. Try watching it over a few weeks to see the shapes change. Record what you see in a notebook.

Phases of Venus

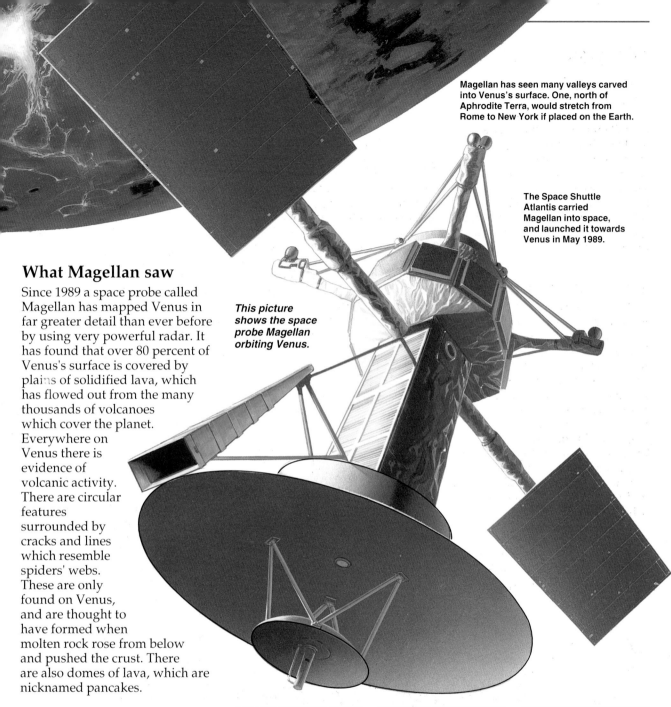

Magellan has seen many valleys carved into Venus's surface. One, north of Aphrodite Terra, would stretch from Rome to New York if placed on the Earth.

The Space Shuttle Atlantis carried Magellan into space, and launched it towards Venus in May 1989.

This picture shows the space probe Magellan orbiting Venus.

What Magellan saw

Since 1989 a space probe called Magellan has mapped Venus in far greater detail than ever before by using very powerful radar. It has found that over 80 percent of Venus's surface is covered by plains of solidified lava, which has flowed out from the many thousands of volcanoes which cover the planet. Everywhere on Venus there is evidence of volcanic activity. There are circular features surrounded by cracks and lines which resemble spiders' webs. These are only found on Venus, and are thought to have formed when molten rock rose from below and pushed the crust. There are also domes of lava, which are nicknamed pancakes.

The craters of Venus

Venus has many craters blasted out of its lava-covered surface, but they look different to those found on other planets. Venus's very thick atmosphere slows down objects passing through it, so they hit the surface with less force and create shallower craters. Here are some other things that can happen:

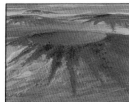

Many craters are circled by splashes. This is rock which was melted by the impact and flowed over the surface.

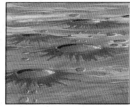

Venus's atmosphere can also shatter incoming objects into pieces, giving many small craters instead of one large one.

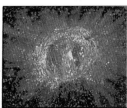

Sometimes the object explodes and no pieces are left. The shock waves leave a dark splotch on the ground.

The Earth and Moon

The Earth is unique in the Solar System because it is the only planet capable of sustaining life. It is in just the right place: it orbits the Sun at an average distance of 149.6 million km (92.9 million mi), which means it is warm enough for water to exist on its surface as a liquid. Water would evaporate if it was too hot and freeze if it was too cold. Earth also has a breathable atmosphere. This, and liquid water, are the two most essential things for the development of life on Earth.

The Earth's atmosphere

From Space, Earth's atmosphere looks like a very thin layer of blue surrounding the planet. It is a thin envelope of nitrogen (77.6%) and oxygen (20.7%). The rest consists of minute traces of many other gases. Earth's atmosphere has the most oxygen of any planet's. This gas is the most vital to life.

Other gases
Oxygen
Nitrogen

Ozone

Some of the Sun's radiation can harm life on Earth. A layer of ozone gas acts as a filter to block most harmful rays. However, scientists have found that man-made gases, chlorofluorocarbons (CFCs), are damaging the ozone layer, and opening up holes in it above the Poles. There is growing concern that unless this stops soon the holes will get larger and lead to an increase in cancers as more radiation reaches living cells.

On this radar photograph the ozone hole is shown pink.

© Nasa / Science Photo Library

The structure of the Earth

Beneath the atmosphere there is a solid surface known as the crust. It is spilt up into large slabs or plates of rock that move and push past each other, creating mountains and other features. Their movement can cause huge earthquakes.

Here you can see the Earth with part cut away. Find out what the different layers are in the diagram to the right.

The Earth takes 365.25 days to orbit the Sun. It takes 23 hours 56 minutes to rotate once.

Its diameter of 12,756km (7,928mi) makes Earth the largest of the Inner Planets.

Photographs of Earth from space show it as different to the other planets. It has lovely blue oceans, and white clouds.

The Earth's crust is between 10 and 50 km (6 and 31mi) deep.

The crust floats on the partly-liquid Mantle. This contains 67% of the Earth's mass and is 2,890km (1,792mi) deep.

The Outer Liquid Core extends down another 2,260 km (1,401 mi) below the surface. It shifts and produces the electric currents which make Earth's magnetic field.

In the middle of the Earth is the Inner Core. This is solid and rich in iron.

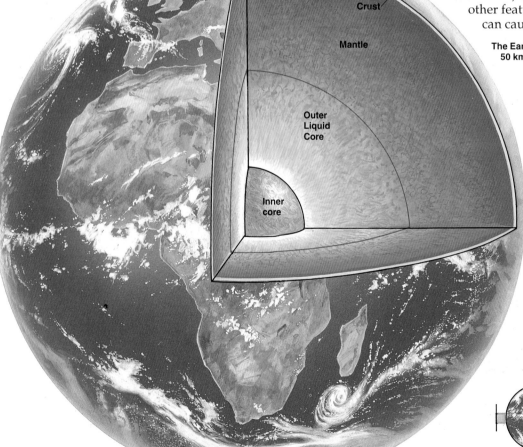

Crust

Mantle

Outer Liquid Core

Inner core

Earth and Moon shown in scale.

Earth   Moon

The Moon

The Earth has just one moon orbiting at an average distance of 376,284km (233,862mi). Some astronomers call this moon Luna (Latin for Moon), but everyone else knows it simply as The Moon.

The Far Side

Earth's gravity has gradually slowed the Moon's rotation until it now takes exactly the same time to orbit the Earth as it does to spin around once. This "synchronous rotation" means we only see one side of the Moon from Earth. The Far Side has only been seen by probes and astronauts.

The Moon spins as it orbits Earth.

The same side faces Earth all the time.

The Moon's shape

As the Moon orbits the Earth, the Sun illuminates a different amount of it every night. Below you can see what the Moon looks like at different times from one point on Earth.

The Sun is shining from this direction.

The pictures below show what the Moon looks like from Earth when it is in each of the numbered positions above.

1. No (or New) Moon
2. Crescent Moon
3. Half Moon (First Quarter)
4. Waxing (Growing)
5. Full Moon
6. Waning (Shrinking)
7. Half Moon (Last quarter)
8. Crescent Moon

A double planet?

The Earth's Moon is unusually large when compared to the size of its parent planet. With a diameter across its equator (middle) of 3,475km (2,160mi), it is only just under a quarter the size of Earth. Because of this, some astronomers think that the Earth and Moon system should really be thought of as a double planet.

Where did the Moon come from?

The Moon's biggest mystery is that we still don't know where it actually came from. Astronomers used to think it was formed at the same time as Earth, around 5 billion years ago. But the rocks collected by Apollo astronauts showed puzzling differences between the Earth and Moon.

Perhaps the early Earth had a system of beautiful rings like Saturn's, and the Moon formed out of them?

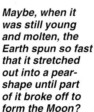

Earth
Moon
Rings

Maybe, when it was still young and molten, the Earth spun so fast that it stretched out into a pear-shape until part of it broke off to form the Moon?

Moon
Earth

Another theory is that when Earth was young it was struck by an object half its size. The impact sent a huge amount of material off into space which formed the Moon.

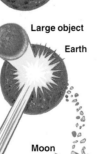

Large object
Earth
Moon

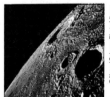

Many of the Moon's large craters are surrounded by bright lines or rays.

The thousands of craters on its face reveal that the Moon had a violent past.

The surface of the Moon

However it formed, we know that the Moon's craters were made when huge pieces of rock struck its surface. The Moon has some of the largest craters in the Solar System. You can see some of them with just your naked eyes.

Copernicus is 97km (60mi) wide.

© Nasa / Science Photo Library

The lunar seas

Some objects struck the Moon so hard they broke the crust. Lava flooded up from below and spread out over the surface. It cooled and hardened to form the dark plains which are visible to the naked eye, and are known as seas.

The future

The American Apollo flights ended in 1972, but astronauts could return to the Moon by 2005, to build large telescopes and a manned Moonbase for teams from many countries. Perhaps it could be used as a staging post for missions to other planets?

Mars

Mars is the fourth planet from the Sun, and is only half the size of the Earth. In some ways it is quite like Earth. It has seasons and its day is just over half an hour longer; but because it lies at an average distance of 227.4 million km (141.3 million mi) from the Sun its surface temperature averages -28 degrees Centigrade (-6 degrees Fahrenheit), and it takes nearly 687 days to orbit the Sun.

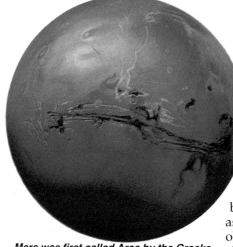

Mars was first called Ares by the Greeks, after their God of War. The Roman word for Ares was Mars.

What Mars looks like

To your naked eye Mars looks like a bright, orange-red star. To see Mars as a disc, and to see any features on its surface, requires a telescope. The first accurate telescopic observations of Mars were made by the astronomer Huygens in 1659. By the 19th century, astronomers had noticed Mars had vague dark areas which appeared to change in size and brightness with the passing of the Martian seasons. Some astronomers assumed that they were patches of vegetation, evidence that there were living things on Mars.

The myth of the canals

In 1877, the astronomer Schiaparelli saw narrow, dark markings on Mars which he thought looked like rivers, so he called them channels, which is *canali* in Italian. Unfortunately, this was mistranslated into English as canals, which suggested they had been built by living creatures. American astronomer Percival Lowell, who observed Mars from 1896 to 1916, also saw the "canals".

© US Geological Survey / Science Photo Library

These are some of the channels on Mars.

Lowell suggested that at some time thirsty Martians had dug canals to carry water from Mars's poles to their cities.

Mars is a frozen, dusty world of craters, volcanoes and canyons, with an atmosphere of mostly carbon dioxide. The atmospheric pressure (how much the gases of the atmosphere press against the planet) is too low to keep water on the surface - it just evaporates away.

The landscape is a desolate plain of undulating orange and brown sand-dunes, blown by the winds and littered with rocks and jagged boulders.

From Mars, the weak, yellow Sun looks just two thirds the size it does from the Earth. Grains of dust suspended in the air scatter the sunlight and turn Mars's sky pink.

The American Viking 2 Lander touched down on Utopia Plain, Mars, in August 1976.

The War of the Worlds

The idea of Martians quickly took hold and in 1898, British author H.G. Wells wrote a book, *The War of the Worlds*, in which Martians attacked Earth with three-legged machines and death rays. In 1938, American radio broadcast a version of it as if it was real. There was panic across the country.

Why is Mars red?

The dried-up rivers and channels which snake across its rocky plains for vast distances show that Mars was once warm enough and had enough atmosphere for water to flow freely on its surface. It maybe even had a huge ocean until an unknown event stripped Mars of its atmosphere and turned its iron-rich soil rust-red.

Space probes to Mars

The US Mariner 4 probe took the first photographs of Mars in 1965. They showed the dark areas were not vegetation and there was no sign of any canals or Martian cities either. Instead, there were just volcanoes, bone-dry dust plains and craters .

Other Mariners found a towering, extinct volcano - Olympus Mons - three times higher than Mount Everest and 600km (373mi) wide; and a huge valley 4,500km (2,800mi) long and 600 km (373mi) wide. It was named Valles Marineris (Mariner Valley).

Mariner 4

In 1976, two Viking probes went to see if life forms such as bacteria or lichen existed on Mars. They took pictures from orbit, and a part of them landed by parachute to take close-ups.

Moons of Mars

Asaph Hall discovered two tiny moons around Mars in 1877. Viking photographs showed us some details: Phobos is 27x22x28km (16x14x17mi) and orbits at a distance of 6,000km (3,730mi). It has a 5km (3mi) wide crater called Stickney and is deeply grooved. Deimos measures 15x12x10km (9x7x6mi) and orbits at 20,000km (12,430mi). Both are very dark and dusty. Many experts think they are from another part of the Solar System and were captured by Mars's gravitational pull.

Deimos

Phobos

Today we know more about Mars's surface than we do about the floor of Earth's oceans.

If life existed on Mars in the past, there may be fossils left behind for future explorers to find.

In the future

Enthusiasts hope that by 2030 the first humans should set foot on Mars. Later missions could build bases which will grow larger until Mars becomes a launching pad for missions further into space.

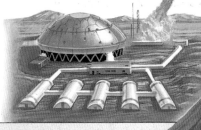

Viking scooped up soil samples to test for signs of life. Some chemical reactions occurred, but the tests were inconclusive.

The asteroids

Asteroids are large pieces of rock and metal left over from the formation of the Solar System five billion years ago. Because they orbit the Sun like the planets, but are much smaller, they are also known as minor planets. Some asteroids have long, looping orbits which take them far away from the Sun. Others follow planets like dogs, but most lie between Mars and Jupiter in The Asteroid Belt.

Seeing asteroids

Most asteroids are too small and faint to see without a telescope, but you can see a few with binoculars. They only ever look like stars from Earth.

This is an asteroid seen from Earth. It has a trail because it moved while the picture was being taken.

Finding the first asteroid

By 1800, astronomers were looking for a planet between Mars and Jupiter. They had found that the planets' distances from the Sun followed a mathematical sequence. It told them that a planet was "missing" here, and where to expect another planet beyond Saturn. Six of the searchers became known as the "Celestial Police".

Here's the sequence: 0,3,6,12,24,48,96. Each number (after 3) is twice the one before. Add 4 to each one and see how close it is to the planets' actual relative distances from the Sun, shown below. The sequence is called Bode's Law after the astronomer who first realized its significance.

Here you can see part of the Asteroid Belt.

Ceres

No planet could be found in the right place, but on the first day of 1801 Piazzi found something in almost exactly the place predicted by Bode's Law. But instead of a planet he had found a much smaller object, which he called Ceres. As many more objects like it were found, astronomers gave them the name "asteroids".

Ceres is a huge chunk of rock 940km (584mi) wide. It takes 4.6 years to orbit the Sun.

Different types

Carbonaceous asteroids like Ceres are very common, stony and darker than coal.

Silicaceous asteroids are fairly bright, metal-bearing stony bodies.

Metallic asteroids may be the exposed, metallic cores of much larger bodies.

Other asteroids

Apart from the asteroids found in the main Belt there are several other groups. The Trojans have the same orbit as Jupiter but circle ahead of and behind it. They are named after characters in the Trojan War, a terrible conflict from Ancient Greek history.

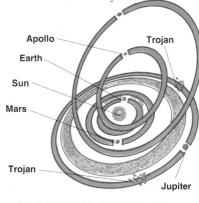

Apollo — Trojan — Earth — Sun — Mars — Trojan — Jupiter

Apollo asteroids lie further from the Sun than Earth but their orbits sometimes cross our planet's path.

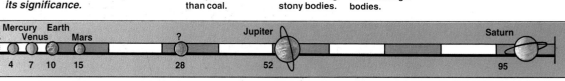

Mercury	Venus	Earth	Mars	?	Jupiter			Saturn
4	7	10	15	28	52			95

Chiron: comet or asteroid?

American, Charles Kowal discovered Chiron in 1977. Its eccentric orbit takes it between 8.5 and 18.5 times further from the Sun than Earth. This behaviour is more like a comet (see pages 26-27) than an asteroid. In 1988 Chiron suddenly grew much brighter and developed a gassy cloud like a comet. Many astronomers now think it is a comet with a diameter of 100-300km (62-186mi). Others think it may be a missing link between comets and asteroids. Maybe as comets grow older and shrink they lose their gas and ice and become asteroids?

Gaspra

In November 1991, the US space probe Galileo took the first close-up photographs of an asteroid when it flew past Gaspra on its way to Jupiter.
They showed it is a dark and irregular object 20km (12mi) wide. It is covered with craters, and it appears that large pieces have been knocked off it in places, perhaps during collisions

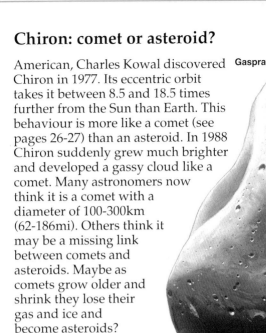

Gaspra

Gaspra is a dark reddish-brown, with lighter patches of grey and blue.

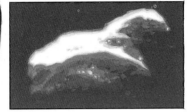

Galileo

with other asteroids, which may be quite common. Recently the photographs were processed to bring out even more detail, and they showed long grooves running across Gaspra like the ones seen on Mars's moon, Phobos. This may be evidence that Mars's moons are captured asteroids.

Future plans

Radar was used to take pictures of an asteroid called Toutatis as it flew past Earth. They showed it is really two heavily-cratered asteroids almost touching each other.
Further radar observations of asteroids are planned soon.

The asteroid Toutatis

Early in the next century, space-probes should fly close to some asteroids to study them. Others will bring samples back to Earth to help prepare for manned expeditions. Because asteroids contain valuable minerals and metals they are an important natural resource for the future. Astronauts may eventually bring them back to Earth and mine them.

This is what a mining operation on an asteroid might look like.

Jupiter

Jupiter, the largest planet in the Solar System, is the fifth from the Sun. Everything about it is huge. Its family of 16 moons makes it like a miniature Solar System. Its diameter of 143,884km (89,424mi) means it is over 11 times wider than Earth.

Jupiter orbits 778 million km (483 million mi) from the Sun, over five times further away than Earth.

Earth

One orbit takes
11.86 Earth years.

Sun

Jupiter

Observing Jupiter

To the naked eye Jupiter looks like a bright star. Because it is so big, even small telescopes show the tinted cloud bands and the Great Red Spot (see right) on its disc.

This is Jupiter through binoculars.

Jupiter through a small telescope.

Moon watching

If they were not so close to Jupiter, the Galilean Moons (see opposite) would be visible to the naked eye. Try looking at them through binoculars (monthly astronomy magazines will tell you where to look). They form a different pattern each night, at times all to one side of the planet, then on both sides.

The structure of Jupiter

Jupiter looks different to the other planets because it is made almost entirely out of gas, like a miniature Sun, with just a tiny, rocky core. When you look at Jupiter you see only the cloud-tops of its 1000km (620mi) thick, multi-toned atmosphere. This atmosphere, which consists mostly of hydrogen and helium, covers the planet like an ocean of gas, and the heat rising from the many layers beneath creates violent storms within it.

Here you can see Jupiter's layers.

Dark, horizontal bands which cross the planet are really gaps in the rising clouds and storms through which you can see deeper, hotter layers of the planet's turbulent atmosphere.

Exploring Jupiter

On December 3rd 1973, Pioneer 10 reached Jupiter and beamed back sensational pictures of its clouds. Voyager probes in 1979 found that Jupiter had three rings, too fine to be seen from Earth. In 1995 the Galileo probe will reach Jupiter. Its main part will orbit the planet taking thousands of photographs while a smaller probe will descend through the clouds of the atmosphere, taking measurements.

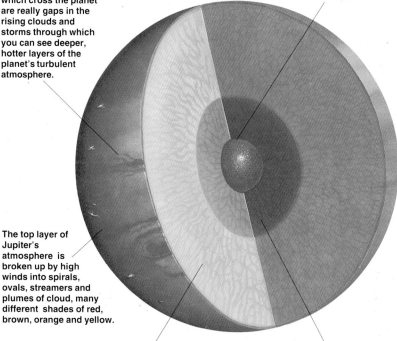

Deep in the middle of the planet there is a solid, rocky core slightly larger than the Earth.

The top layer of Jupiter's atmosphere is broken up by high winds into spirals, ovals, streamers and plumes of cloud, many different shades of red, brown, orange and yellow.

Beneath Jupiter's atmosphere is a 17,000km (10,565mi) thick layer where the hydrogen gas is compressed so much it is more like a liquid.

The ocean of "liquid hydrogen" surrounds a layer where hydrogen is compressed so much more that it acts like a metal. This layer of "metallic hydrogen" makes up over 77% of the mass of Jupiter.

Callisto		Ganymede
1,880,000km (1,168,428mi)		1,070,000km (665,009mi)

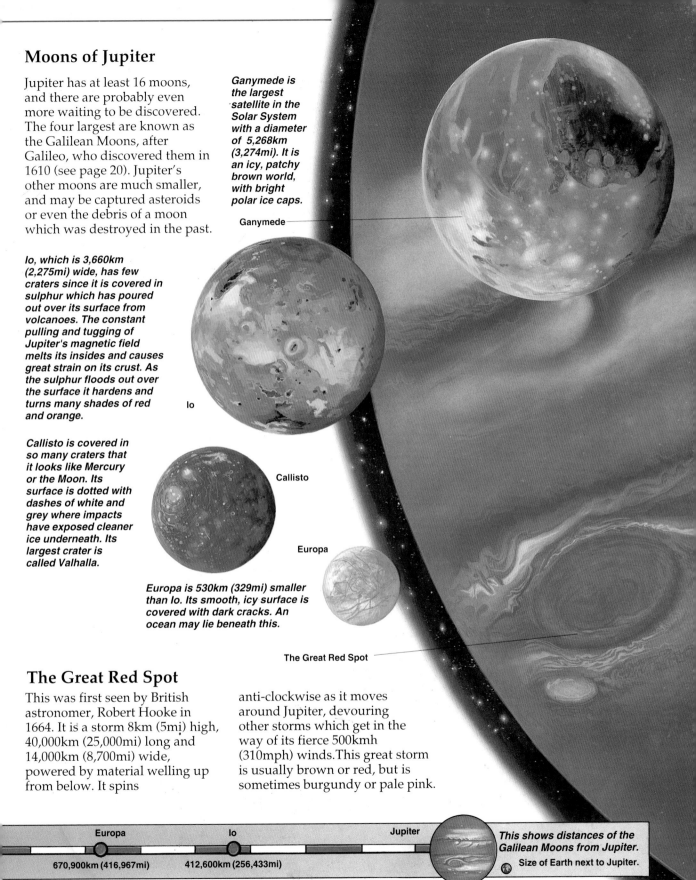

Moons of Jupiter

Jupiter has at least 16 moons, and there are probably even more waiting to be discovered. The four largest are known as the Galilean Moons, after Galileo, who discovered them in 1610 (see page 20). Jupiter's other moons are much smaller, and may be captured asteroids or even the debris of a moon which was destroyed in the past.

Io, which is 3,660km (2,275mi) wide, has few craters since it is covered in sulphur which has poured out over its surface from volcanoes. The constant pulling and tugging of Jupiter's magnetic field melts its insides and causes great strain on its crust. As the sulphur floods out over the surface it hardens and turns many shades of red and orange.

Callisto is covered in so many craters that it looks like Mercury or the Moon. Its surface is dotted with dashes of white and grey where impacts have exposed cleaner ice underneath. Its largest crater is called Valhalla.

Ganymede is the largest satellite in the Solar System with a diameter of 5,268km (3,274mi). It is an icy, patchy brown world, with bright polar ice caps.

Ganymede

Io

Callisto

Europa

Europa is 530km (329mi) smaller than Io. Its smooth, icy surface is covered with dark cracks. An ocean may lie beneath this.

The Great Red Spot

The Great Red Spot

This was first seen by British astronomer, Robert Hooke in 1664. It is a storm 8km (5mi) high, 40,000km (25,000mi) long and 14,000km (8,700mi) wide, powered by material welling up from below. It spins anti-clockwise as it moves around Jupiter, devouring other storms which get in the way of its fierce 500kmh (310mph) winds. This great storm is usually brown or red, but is sometimes burgundy or pale pink.

Europa

Io

Jupiter

670,900km (416,967mi)

412,600km (256,433mi)

This shows distances of the Galilean Moons from Jupiter.

Size of Earth next to Jupiter.

Saturn

Saturn is the second largest planet in the Solar System, and the sixth in order from the Sun. Like Jupiter, it is made almost entirely out of gas. Saturn is often called the Ringed Planet because it is encircled by a system of beautiful rings almost five times as wide as the planet itself. Saturn is the most distant planet easily visible to the naked eye. It looks like a bright, golden star. A telescope is needed to see its discs or rings.

Timetable of discovery

1633: Gassendi sketches an unknown bright ring around Saturn.
1656: Huygens publishes sketches of Saturn by various people. Declares that Saturn has "a thin flat ring" that does not touch the planet.
1675: Cassini finds a gap in the rings: named the Cassini Division after him.
1837: Encke finds a second gap.
1850: Astronomers find the C Ring.

1852: Lassell discovers the C Ring is almost transparent, so it cannot be solid; it is probably particles so close together they look like a solid band.
1857: James Clerk Maxwell proves mathematically that solid rings orbiting Saturn would be torn apart.
1895: Keeler finds that ring sections rotate at different speeds, which proves the rings cannot be solid.

Here you can see Saturn and its rings. Saturn's diameter of 120,660km (74,990mi) makes it nine times wider than Earth.

Saturn lies at an average distance of 1,427 million km (almost 887 million mi) from the Sun. This huge orbit means that it takes over 29 years to crawl once around the Sun.

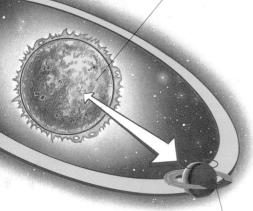

Sun

Saturn has a very low density. That means it is very light. In fact, if you could find an ocean big enough to drop Saturn into, the planet would actually float.

We now know that as Saturn moves around the Sun, the angle and size of the rings changes and they appear to tip up and down. They seem to vanish altogether when they are edge-on to us. This is what was actually happening.

Saturn's day is very short. It takes just 10 hours and 14 minutes to rotate once. That rapid rotation squashes its poles down so it looks like an oval.

Saturn

Lord of the rings

Saturn's rings puzzled early astronomers with their crude equipment. When Galileo (pages 32, 37) first looked at Saturn in 1610 he was amazed to see what looked like a moon on each side, as if it was a triple planet. Two years later the moons seemed to have vanished.

Galileo made drawings of his observations, like this.

When Galileo first saw the rings his telescope was not powerful enough to show them properly. They looked like discs.

The moons seemed to vanish when Galileo viewed the rings edge-on, like this.

The rings start to open up again as Saturn tilts.

The rings seen at their best, tilted towards us.

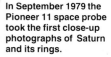
In September 1979 the Pioneer 11 space probe took the first close-up photographs of Saturn and its rings.

The rings revealed

The Voyager probes found that each of the major rings consists of thousands of smaller rings. All the rings are identified by letters. Some of them, like the F Ring, are kinked and knotted like twisted ropes. Others are not quite central. Particles in the rings range from tiny, dust-sized grains to large ice boulders.

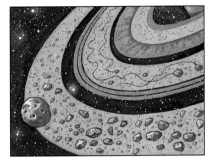

Outer ring particles are kept in place, like a flock of sheep, by tiny satellites called Shepherd Moons which orbit inside and outside of them.

The spokes

The Voyagers also discovered mysterious spokes rotating around Saturn inside the bright B Ring. It seems these are made out of fine dust which is lifted up above the rings and carried around Saturn by its magnetic field. Some people have now seen the spokes with telescopes.

Saturn's satellites

Like Jupiter, Saturn has many moons, a few of which can be seen from Earth. Being so far from the Sun, most of them are balls of very hard ice. Almost all are covered with craters, and most have valleys and mountains too.

Mimas

Mimas is 392km (244mi) wide and is covered in craters. The impact which created its largest crater nearly blasted the moon apart.

Enceladus is slightly larger than Mimas and is much smoother. Most of its craters have been covered over by flows of ice.

Enceladus

Tethys

Tethys is much larger than Enceladus. Craters and long valleys cover its surface. The longest valley, Ithaca, is 2000km (1,243mi) long.

Titan

Saturn's most important moon is Titan. It is bigger than Mercury, with a thick atmosphere. It is more like a small planet than a moon. Later this decade, a European probe will be dropped into its atmosphere, from the US spaceprobe Cassini.

In 1980 and 1981, Voyager probes saw smaller versions of Jupiter's Great Red Spot, but found that most features in Saturn's atmosphere were hidden by a layer of haze.

We now know there are four planets in the Solar System with rings. Saturn's are by far the most easily-seen and beautiful.

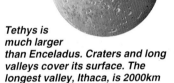

Odysseus, on Tethys, is one of the largest craters in the Solar System. It is 400km (249mi) wide.

Uranus and Neptune

Beyond Saturn's orbit lies a pair of planets with much in common - Uranus and Neptune.

Uranus

Uranus was found by British astronomer William Herschel in 1781. It had been observed twice before but had not been recognised as a planet. Uranus's average distance from the Sun of 2,869 million km (1,783 million mi) means it is 19 times further from it than Earth. It takes just over 84 years to orbit the Sun once.

Observing Uranus and Neptune

At its brightest Uranus can just be glimpsed as a star with the naked eye. Neptune cannot be seen with the eye, and binoculars show it as just a star. Even powerful telescopes only show it as a small, bluish disc.

The rolling planet

Uranus is unique in that it orbits the Sun on its side, rolling like a barrel, so its poles face us alternately. A huge comet may have struck it millions of years ago, tipping it sideways.

Uranus rolls like this.

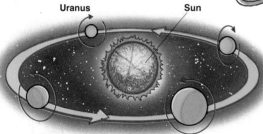

Uranus   Sun

The rings of Uranus

Uranus's faint rings were found in 1977 when astronomers looking at a star pass behind Uranus saw it wink five minutes earlier than expected. Something had blocked its light, perhaps a moon. When it happened on the other side, too, they knew they had found some rings.

This is Uranus (on the left) and Neptune (on the right). Both planets are around four times wider than Earth. They have thick atmospheres and small, rocky cores. Both have ring systems and a family of icy moons.

The moons of Uranus

Uranus has five main moons. Both Ariel and Umbriel are dark and cratered. Titania has deep, long valleys. One, Messina Chasmata, runs for 1,500km (932mi). Heavily cratered Oberon has not been seen well yet. Tiny Miranda is a 472km (293mi) wide ball of battered ice.

Ariel

Umbriel

Titania

Oberon

Miranda

Some astronomers think Miranda has been blown apart by comets or asteroids, making a chaotic, jagged landscape.

These amazing cliffs of ice on Miranda are over 20km (12mi) high.

Neptune

Like Uranus, Neptune was seen and recorded by several people before it was discovered to be a planet in 1846. It was the first planet to be found by mathematical calculation, after it was seen that Uranus was being pulled at by a more distant object and people tried to discover what it could be.

Neptune is 30 times further from the Sun than Earth. It takes 165 years to make one complete orbit of the Sun.

Changing places

Because Pluto's orbit sometimes cuts inside the orbit of Neptune, Neptune is sometimes the furthest planet from the Sun. It will be until 1999, when Pluto will regain its title of most distant planet from the Sun.

Pluto

Sun

Neptune

Pluto's orbit cuts inside Neptune's.

Neptune is a breathtaking blue. It is blue because its thick methane atmosphere is good at reflecting blue light.

Neptune's rings

Before Voyager 2 reached Neptune, observations from Earth had suggested that the planet was surrounded by a system of arcs or incomplete rings. The probe found five complete rings which were so dark only the probe's cameras could see them. The arc turned out to be a thick lump of material in the outermost ring.

The atmosphere has bands of darker cloud and a storm called the Great Dark Spot. It is 8km (5mi) wide and 12km (7.4mi) long.

Voyager found streamers of wispy cloud and oval-shaped storms racing around Neptune, driven by some of the strongest winds in the Solar System.

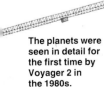

The planets were seen in detail for the first time by Voyager 2 in the 1980s.

Triton

Neptune's main moons are Triton and Nereid. Nereid has not been clearly seen yet but Triton is a fascinating moon. It is 2,705km (1,681mi) wide, and orbits Neptune backwards. Most of its surface is bright and smooth. The ice around its south pole is pink and it has a thin atmosphere.

Neptune

Triton

Voyager's cameras saw dark streaks on Triton, which astronomers think formed like this.

Liquid nitrogen may lie below the icy surface of Triton.

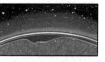

It explodes through the crust in a shower of ice and gas, like a geyser.

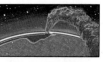

The debris is carried downwind and falls to the ground in dark streaks.

Voyager 2's discoveries

Almost all our knowledge of Neptune came from the Voyager 2 spaceprobe's fly-past of 1989. Because it is even further from the Sun than boring, green Uranus astronomers suspected Neptune would be even less interesting. They were wrong. Voyager 2 showed it is one of the most beautiful planets in the Solar System.

Pluto and Planet X

A fter the discovery that something was pulling at Uranus and Neptune from outside their orbits, Pluto was found in 1930 after a long search by American astronomer, Clyde Tombaugh.

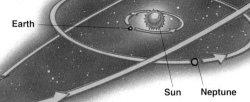

Pluto's minimum distance from the Sun is 4,425 million km (2,750 million mi).

Earth

Pluto's maximum distance from the Sun is 7,375 million km (4,583 million mi).

Sun   Neptune

Pluto

Pluto, planet or not?

There is great debate about whether Pluto is a planet at all. It certainly doesn't behave like one. Pluto's looping orbit is more like a comet's. The furthest point in its orbit takes Pluto fifty times further from the Sun than Earth.

Pluto's years

Pluto's orbit is so huge that it takes 248 of our years to go once around the Sun. If Pluto rotates once every 6 days 9 hours, how many Pluto days are there in its year? Answer on page 35.

Because Pluto is so far away it is very hard to see. The most powerful telescopes only show it as a tiny disc with no markings on its surface.

What is Pluto really like?

Recent observations using the most advanced technology suggest Pluto may be similar to Neptune's moon, Triton. Pluto's diameter is around 2,300km (1,429mi), slightly smaller than Triton, and both have bright and dark areas.

Pluto seems to have a surface of frozen methane and nitrogen ice, bright poles and a thin atmosphere.

Pluto's moon

In 1978, Pluto's only moon was discovered. It is so large compared to Pluto that the two are almost a double planet.

Pluto and Charon through a telescope

The moon, Charon, was found when astronomers examining a photograph of Pluto saw that the planet looked elongated. Later observations confirmed that there was a moon orbiting close to Pluto.

Pluto

Experts now think that Pluto's moon, Charon, is more than half the size of Pluto.

Charon

Charon orbits Pluto at an average distance of 19,640km (12,206mi).

Earth

Earth's Moon   Pluto   Charon

This shows the relative sizes and distances apart of Earth and Moon and Pluto and Charon.

The quest for planet X

Because Pluto has been shown in calculations to be too small to affect the orbits of Uranus and Neptune seriously, some astronomers believe there is a tenth planet out there, waiting to be found, which might be responsible. There was a false alarm in 1992 when two astronomers using telescopes in Hawaii discovered a new object far beyond Pluto.

View of the Keck telescope on Mauna Kea, Hawaii, at sunset.

The object, called 1992 QB1, proved to have a diameter of approximately 200km (124mi) and was too small to be a genuine planet. 1992 QB1's nickname is Smiley. In 1993 a second mini-planet, Karla, was found. Karla is very similar to 1992 QB1 but is even further away from the Sun.

Solar System spies

Smiley got its nick-name because its discoverers were reading a book by British writer John Le Carré at the time. It was called *Tinker, Tailor, Soldier, Spy*, and is about a spy called Smiley and his arch-enemy, Karla.

Mini-planets galore

Even though they are not genuine planets, Smiley and Karla are still very important. Before they were found, the Dutch astronomer Kuiper had suggested that there may be a belt containing a large number of small, icy bodies out at the edge of the Solar System. It was named the Kuiper Belt after him. Smiley and Karla may well be the first members of the Kuiper Belt to be discovered. One theory says that if Planet X does exist, it may lie twice as far from the Sun as Pluto. It may be in an orbit which takes it far above, and then below, the orbits of the other planets. Its year may be as much as 600 Earth years long. Some astronomers say, however, that the existence of the smaller objects that have been found makes the possibility of there being a large, tenth planet less likely.

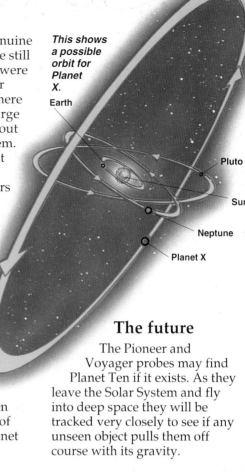

This shows a possible orbit for Planet X.

Earth

Pluto

Sun

Neptune

Planet X

The future

The Pioneer and Voyager probes may find Planet Ten if it exists. As they leave the Solar System and fly into deep space they will be tracked very closely to see if any unseen object pulls them off course with its gravity.

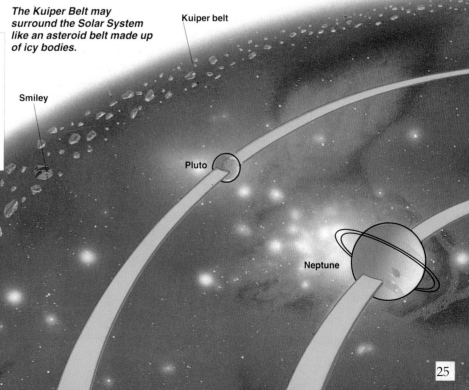

The Kuiper Belt may surround the Solar System like an asteroid belt made up of icy bodies.

Kuiper belt

Smiley

Pluto

Neptune

Comets and meteoroids

As well as its many planets, moons and asteroids, the Solar System contains many thousands of smaller icy bodies which are debris left over from its birth.

Comets

Comets are like huge, dirty snowballs which orbit the Sun and they are usually named after the person or the people who first discover them. They are very different to planets: their orbits are much more elliptical, so they spend most of their time far away from the Sun and only come near it for a brief time. When they approach the Sun they become warm and melt and may grow a tail of gas and dust.

Bright comets like this occasionally stretch across almost the whole sky.

The solid, central part, called the nucleus, is made of frozen gas and ice, gritty dust and larger rocks.

Some comets have highly inclined orbits which take them far above or below the rest of the Solar System over thousands of years.

Here are the orbits of some well-known comets.

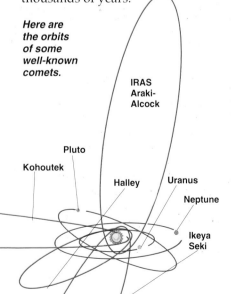

IRAS Araki-Alcock

Pluto

Kohoutek

Halley

Uranus

Neptune

Ikeya Seki

What do comets look like?

Most comets are less than 10km (6mi)wide, but many can still be seen from Earth with the naked eye when they are near the Sun. They usually look like tiny smudges of grey light. Occasionally, a very bright comet appears with a long, silvery tail which cuts across the sky like a searchlight.

Comets' glowing tails are often broken up into plumes and streamers,with delicate twists and swirls along them.

Astronomers now know that comets are mountains of dirty ice. They may come from a huge "shell" around the Solar System, and contain material formed at its birth. Below you can see how the tail of a comet forms.

This is a comet flying through space toward the Sun. At this stage it has no tail.

As the comet nears the Sun, it melts and gas and dust stream out into space forming a cloud which is called the coma.

A constant stream of particles from the Sun, called the Solar Wind, blows some of the coma out behind to form the famous tail.

Are all comets the same?

A comet's Period is how long it takes to orbit the Sun. Comets taking between 3.3 and 150 years are called Periodical. Others, which can take many thousands of years, are Non-Periodical. It is impossible to predict when Non-Periodical comets will appear because they have never been recorded before.

Halley's Comet

British astronomer, Edmund Halley noticed a comet he saw in 1682 was similar to ones seen in 1531 and 1607 (about 76 years apart). Most astronomers thought it was a new comet each time. Halley thought it was the same one, and predicted it would return in1758. He died in 1742, but the comet did reappear 16 years later.

A comet seen in 1066 at the Battle of Hastings, and woven into the Bayeux Tapestry, may have been Halley's.

People used to think comets were bad omens, foretelling war and destruction and the deaths of kings and emperors.

De Chéseaux Comet

Meteoroids

The Solar System is full of much smaller pieces of space debris than comets, called meteoroids. These may be grains of dust from comets, large chunks of rock or even fragments of shattered asteroids.

Shooting stars

Occasionally, Earth crosses the paths of these meteoroids and they burn up as they plummet through the atmosphere in a streak of light which is called a meteor, or a shooting star.

Earth

Earth's atmosphere

Meteoroid

Once the meteoroid enters Earth's atmosphere, it becomes a meteor.

The Halley spaceprobe

Halley's most recent visit was in 1986, when it was just visible to the naked eye. It was not clearly seen from Earth but several space probes caught up with it as it raced in toward the Sun and returned the first ever close-up pictures.

Halley's icy nucleus is peanut-shaped, 15km (8mi) long and 8km (5mi) wide.

The best pictures were taken by the European Giotto probe. They showed craters, mountains and ridges and huge fountains of gas and dust gushing from cracks in Halley's coal-black sides.

Comet records

The largest comet coma ever recorded was that of the Great Comet of 1811. It was 3.2 million km (2 million mi) wide, which made it even larger than the Sun. The Great Comet of 1843 had the longest tail ever seen so far: It was long enough to stretch from the Sun to Mars. The most-tailed comet on record is De Chéseaux Comet of 1744. It had at least six bright tails. The longest Period record belongs to Delevan's Comet, last seen in 1914 - it may be 24 million years.

The future

Future spaceprobes will land on comets to take samples. Many experts believe that comets are related to asteroids and tests will prove it. Scientists also think comets may be rich in organic matter, which contains the building blocks of life. Some even believe it was a comet that brought life to Earth.

You can see a few meteors every hour on a clear night; but when Earth passes through the stream of dust left behind by a passing comet, dozens may be visible every hour for a very short time.

This photograph, taken on 17th November 1966, shows the Leonid meteor shower. At its height, 40,000 meteors were seen in 40 minutes.

© Dennis Milon / Science Photo Library

Two tails

Comets can actually have two tails: a straight, blue gas tail which stretches behind the comet, always pointing away from the Sun; and a yellow, dust tail curving out behind the comet, tracing out its orbital path.

Here you can see a comet's two tails.

© Royer & Padilla/Science Photo Library

Above is Comet West, photographed on 9th March 1976, stretching across the night sky.

Dust tail

Sun

Gas tail

Stones from space

The pieces of meteoroids which survive their plunge through the atmosphere as meteors and fall to the ground as charred rocks are called meteorites. They are usually dark and very heavy, often looking rusted in places.
Even though meteorites have crashed through house roofs and into gardens, the chances of being hit by one are very remote.

The Milky Way and beyond

The Sun, all the stars you can see in the night sky, and a hundred thousand million more, are all members of a huge system of stars called a galaxy. There are millions of other galaxies of different sizes and shapes scattered throughout space, separated from each other by vast, empty gulfs.

Where is the Solar System?

Once, Ancient astronomers thought the Earth was central to everything that exists in space. Today they know that our Solar System lies out near the edge of the Milky Way, which itself is just one among countless galaxies, so Earth is not the middle point as was thought.

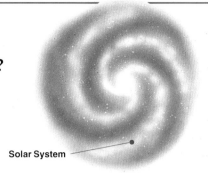

Solar System

This shows the approximate position of the Solar System in the Milky Way Galaxy.

What does a galaxy look like?

A third of all galaxies are spirals. They have bright middles and several curved arms of stars.

Elliptical galaxies are lens-shaped masses of old, red stars which contain little gas or dust.

Irregular galaxies don't really have any shape at all. They are just like clouds of stars.

Hovering above and below the Galaxy are over one hundred huge star clusters. Each globular cluster, as they are called, contains up to a million stars.

From high above, our Galaxy would look like a Catherine Wheel, with glowing arms made of millions of hot, young blue stars, curving away from its yellow-orange middle.

The Milky Way

Our galaxy is usually known simply as The Galaxy, though it is often referred to as the Milky Way Galaxy as well. It is a spiral. However, some astronomers have suggested it might be a barred spiral. That means it would have just two arms growing out of a central bar which cuts across the middle of it.

If you could see our Galaxy from the side you would see it has central bulge. Some people think it looks like a pair of fried eggs placed back to back.

Clusters of galaxies

Just as stars group together in clusters, galaxies form clusters too, and massive clusters of clusters called superclusters. Our Galaxy is a member of a cluster known as the Local Group which may be five million light years across (see what light years are on the page opposite). It contains around 30 galaxies and ours is one of the two largest ones.

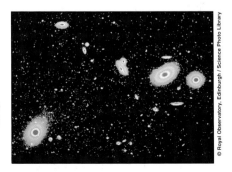

This photograph shows the Virgo cluster of galaxies. It is 50 million light years (see right) away and contains 1,000 galaxies.

Black holes

At the core of the Galaxy, in the middle of a massive ball of ancient red stars, there may lie an enormous black hole: a very dense object with such strong gravity that not even light rays can escape from it. It traps and devours stars like a huge monster.

When a star dies in a huge supernova explosion, only its dense core may survive.

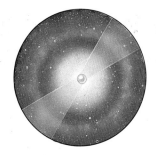

Some become pulsars, which spin very rapidly and flash like lighthouses.

Others become black holes, bottomless pits from which nothing can ever escape.

In some places within the arms there are clouds of glowing pink, green and blue gas. These are nebulae, stellar nurseries where new stars are being born.

In some places there are dark clouds of gas and dust blotting out the light of the stars behind them.

How much can you see?

Astronomers know in which direction the middle of the Galaxy lies because that is where the stars are densest. Looking towards it, you see a great mass of stars that all merge into one misty cloud. Stars spread away from the middle on either side, forming a band of light which stretches across the sky like a wide aircraft trail. This is what people call the Milky Way in the night sky.

© Fred Espenak / Science Photo Library

Though it is best from the southern hemisphere, the misty trail of the Milky Way can be seen anywhere in the world.

What are light years?

Galaxies are staggeringly huge. To use ordinary measures of distance to describe their size is impractical, so astronomers use light years instead. Light is the fastest thing in the Universe. It travels at 300,000km (186,000mi) per second. One light year is the distance light travels in a year: 9.46 million million km (5.88 million million miles). Our Galaxy is 100,000 light years across. Earth lies 30,000 light years from its middle.

Dance of the galaxies

Galaxies rotate slowly. Our own Galaxy takes 230 million years to rotate once, which means that just one Galactic Year ago the dinosaurs were walking on Earth. The Galaxy has rotated fifty two times since its birth.

Diplodocus

Seeing the Milky Way

The best time to see the Milky Way if you live in the northern hemisphere is between July and September. People in the southern hemisphere see it at its best between October and December. Binoculars show it consists of huge numbers of stars.

The story of the Universe

The Universe is everything that exists, from atoms to galaxies. Ever since they began studying the Universe, astronomers have wondered how it formed. They peered out into its depths through telescopes to look for clues to its origin. They found that the galaxies around ours are moving away from us and the Universe is expanding. If that is true, it must once have been much smaller. Some astronomers now have a theory which explains how this might have happened. Although this "Big Bang" theory does not answer all the questions about the origins of the Universe, it does fit astronomers' observations very well.

The Big Bang Theory

According to the Big Bang theory, the Universe was formed in a tremendous, unimaginably violent explosion - the Big Bang itself - over 15 billion years ago. You cannot ask what there was before the Big Bang because everything which exists, or has ever existed, was formed in it; and you cannot ask what happened before the Big Bang either, because time itself started with the Big Bang.

The Big Bang was an explosion of energy. After a fraction of a second it started to cool and form particles called photons which spread out in every direction. The fireball began to cool into a thick soup of atomic particles, forming hydrogen and helium gases.

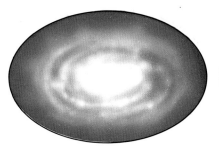

The fireball began to change into a seething, foggy cloud of matter. It was so dense that rays of light could not travel far within it, so it was also very dark. Slowly, the gas atoms collected into vast clumps which heated up and later evolved into the first galaxies.

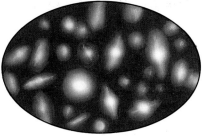

After several thousand years the temperature of the Universe fell to just a few thousand degrees and the fog cleared away. Light could then travel freely, galaxies began to form and the Universe became as transparent as it is today.

Almost ten billion years later, in a galaxy which astronomers would later call the Milky Way, the Sun, Earth and the other planets of our own Solar System were formed. The primitive forms of life which then developed on Earth later evolved into humans.

Where's the proof?

There is very strong evidence to support the Big Bang. For example, if it is correct, the radiation trapped in the early fireball would have weakened and spread out into the background, leaving a very weak "echo" which should be detectable from Earth with radio telescopes. In 1965 just such background radiation was found, coming from every direction in the sky.

In 1992 the COBE satellite found weak "ripples" in the background radiation, as predicted by the Big Bang Theory.

The missing mass

The Universe's fate depends on its mass, or the amount of matter it contains. Most astronomers are convinced that it contains more matter than we can see, and they are now hunting for its "missing mass". It may consist of many objects that are small but very dense and so dark that we cannot see them. Calculations have shown that if the Universe was only made out of the things we can see it would have expanded too quickly after the Big Bang to allow galaxies to form. But because they did form it must have more mass.

We may only be seeing 10% of the Universe.

Invisible

Visible

How will the Universe end?

If not much missing mass is found, the Universe could continue to expand forever. However, if there is a lot more mass, the force of gravity may eventually slow down the expansion altogether, and pull everything backwards until the galaxies collide in a gigantic "Big Crunch".

If nothing gets in the way, a star shines steadily.

If something passes in front of it, its light dims.

As the thing moves on, the star brightens.

Astronomers have made the first observations of objects they think make up at least some of the missing mass. They saw stars briefly and unexpectedly dim, then brighten, as shown in the pictures above, as invisible objects passed in front of them. You can keep up with the latest discoveries and theories on this subject in astronomy and science magazines.

Telescopes past and present

It wasn't until the invention of the telescope that people finally began to make sense of the Universe. Our understanding of the nature and structure of the Universe has evolved and increased as the telescope itself has become more powerful and sophisticated. Telescopes have revolutionized the way we view the Universe and our place in it.

First telescopes

The very first crude telescope was invented in 1608 by a Dutch spectacle maker, Hans Lippershey. It could only magnify objects a few times. The first true astronomical telescope was built by Italian, Galileo, in 1609. It magnified objects up to thirty times and, like Lippershey's it used lenses to refract, or bend, light so it was known as a refractor. Over the next century refractors grew bigger and bigger.

Galileo's first telescopes looked something like this.

By the middle of the 18th century astronomers such as the German, Hevelius were using giant refractors with tubes as long as 46m (150ft) supported by wooden frames. They magnified objects many times and were used mostly to look at the planets.

This is a picture of Hevelius's huge refractor, which he used on the roof of a tall building.

The Dutch astronomer Huygens used a different kind of refractor. His aerial telescope consisted of just a pair of lenses, and no tube.

One lens was mounted on top of a tall mast.

The observer looked into a second lens, fitted to an eyepiece.

The eyepiece was lined up with the other lens with a short cord.

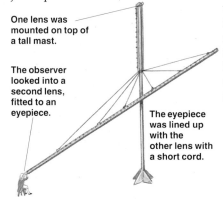

Refractors continued to grow in size. The 101cm (40in) Yerkes refractor, built at Williams Bay in America in 1897, is still the largest refractor in the world.

Reflecting telescopes

In 1668, Sir Isaac Newton invented a new type of telescope which used mirrors instead of lenses. It became known as the Newtonian reflector, and it was a turning point in the science of astronomy. Because mirrors can be made much bigger and more cheaply than lenses, it meant that much larger and more powerful telescopes could be built. All the largest telescopes are reflectors.

This shows how Newton's reflector works.

Light enters here.

Light reflects off the main mirror, back up the tube.

A small, angled mirror sends the light reflected from the main mirror out of a hole in the side. A small eyepiece focuses the light and forms an image.

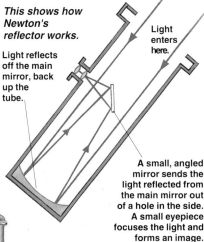

Rosse's Leviathan

By 1845, Ireland's Earl of Rosse had built what was then the world's largest telescope. It is still impressive today. His huge reflector at Birr Castle was nicknamed The Leviathan. Rosse used it to study very faint, distant objects, and discovered the spiral nature of galaxies with it.

This is Rosse's Leviathan.

Radio telescopes

Radio telescopes use very large dishes or aerials (antennas) that collect the faint radio signals given out by objects in space. Radio waves tell us things light waves cannot. In fact, some objects are only "visible" to radio telescopes.

© Tony Craddock / Science Photo Library

Jodrell Bank, England, is the largest steerable radio telescope in the world, with a dish 76.2m (250ft) wide.

Now there are radio telescopes all over the world. Some can be steered towards specific targets while others just point straight up at the sky. Others listen to signals coming from every direction at once.

Radio messages

The largest radio telescope in the world is the huge Arecibo dish in Puerto Rico. The 304.8m (1,000ft) wide bowl is built into the side of a hill. In 1974, Arecibo beamed a simple, coded message describing our planet and civilisation out into space, hoping it will reach any aliens living in a distant star cluster. Any reply will not reach us for many thousands of years.

The Arecibo radio telescope, in Puerto Rico.

The Keck

The largest telescope in the world today is the Keck, built on the summit of the extinct Hawaiian volcano Mauna Kea. Powerful computers ensure it performs to its maximum ability at all times. Its revolutionary design makes it the most powerful telescope ever. It can study an area of the Universe eight times larger than any other telescope, and its huge mirror can observe objects fainter and further away than ever before.

This is Keck, a huge reflector.

Its 1000cm (394in) wide mirror is made of 36 hexagonal segments which act like a single, large mirror.

A second Keck telescope - Keck II - is almost finished. The Kecks will work together to study the Universe in more detail than ever before.

The Hubble Space Telescope

The Hubble Space Telescope (HST) was a dream come true for all the astronomers who had wanted to place telescopes in orbit. They knew that from high above the polluted, shifting atmosphere, telescopes would be able to see much further and more clearly. Unfortunately, soon after the HST was launched, it was found to be sending back blurred images. Its main mirror was misshapen; but after astronauts repaired it in 1993 the HST's images have been breathtaking.

Here is the Hubble Space Telescope in orbit.

The HST is a reflector with a main mirror 2.4m (94.5in) across.

The HST was carried into space in April 1990 by the Space Shuttle Discovery.

Telescopes of the future

Telescopes are getting bigger and bigger. Two of the biggest, after Keck, in the world today are the 508cm (200in) Palomar reflector and the Russian 590cm (232in) reflector. There are plans to build a new generation of even larger ones over the next decade, with multiple small mirrors acting as one large one. The US Large Binocular Telescope will consist of twin 840cm (330in) reflectors. The Very Large Telescope to be built in Chile, will consist of four 800cm (315in) telescopes working together.

About astronomers

Astronomy as a hobby

Thousands of people all over the world - called amateur astronomers or sky-watchers - enjoy observing the sky and learning more about the Universe. It does not cost a lot to start and there are lots of amazing things to see. Simply viewing the sky through binoculars, you can see more interesting details and phenomena.

View through binoculars.

Getting started

All you need to start observing the night sky are your eyes and a clear sky. Although it will take you some time to learn your way around the sky and to recognize objects in it, it's well worth spending the time. If the sky is clear tonight, you could get started straight away, using the star charts on pages 40-47 in this book. A good idea is to ask someone who already knows about the night sky to help you and point things out to you. Astronomical societies are good places to contact enthusiasts who will be glad to help. There are some useful addresses you could contact on the next page.

View through a small telescope.

Once you can recognize the constellations visible from where you live, you will be able to greet them like old friends. Then you can start to look for star clusters, nebulae and galaxies with binoculars or a small telescope.

What to look for

All the things below are visible to the naked eye, but they become harder to see, or rarer, as you go down the list:

Sun	nebulae
Moon	lunar eclipse
stars	solar eclipse
planets	northern or
galaxies	southern lights

You could keep a list and check them off when you see them.

Serious amateurs

The most serious amateur astronomers buy expensive equipment, such as large telescopes, computers and cameras. Some specialize in one subject, such as measuring the brightness of stars, observing the planets or recording meteor showers. Many amateurs know the sky better than some professionals. Some have even discovered asteroids and comets, which are named after them.

Professional astronomers

Some amateurs go on to become professionals and study the Universe as a career. This requires study at a University in science subjects, such as maths and physics. Professionals may never actually look at the sky. Instead, physicists like Stephen Hawking work with long, complicated equations to explain the nature of the Universe and predict its fate.

Astronomers working for NASA, the United States' space agency.

Professionals may use telescopes, but usually by remote control and sometimes from the opposite side of the globe. Professionals work in museums, laboratories and Universities all over the world.

An astronomer at work inside the Solar Vacuum Telescope at Kitt Peak National Observatory, Arizona, USA.

Some work in airborne observatories or go on expeditions, gathering meteorites in the Antarctic or watching solar eclipses from the rainforests of South America, for example. Some help design and control space probes. Others explore the depths of the Universe with the Hubble Space Telescope and observe exploding stars, colliding galaxies and planets being formed. If an unexpected event occurs, such as the appearance of a bright comet or supernova, amateurs and professionals work side by side and share their results.

Taking simple photographs

It is easy to take simple photographs of the night sky. What you need is a 35mm SLR camera which can take time exposures and a 400ASA film.

Mount the camera on a tripod, fit it with a cable release and focus it on infinity. Aim the lens at the night sky. Good subjects would be a constellation such as Orion, the Moon or a bright planet.

Start to take an exposure by pressing the release. Count to 15, then press again. Your photographs will show the stars as bright points of light. Longer exposures will show the stars as streaks or trails.

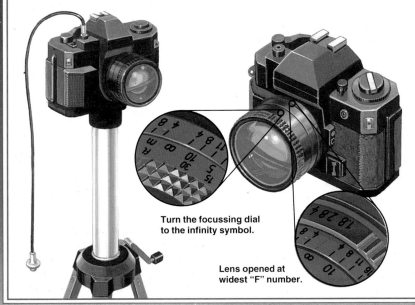

Turn the focussing dial to the infinity symbol.

Lens opened at widest "F" number.

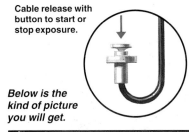

Cable release with button to start or stop exposure.

Below is the kind of picture you will get.

© John Sanford / Science Photo Library

Useful addresses

Australia
Sydney Observatory, Observatory Hill, Sydney 2000
Perth Observatory, Walnut Rd., Bickley WA 6076

Or look up in your telephone directory:
The Astronomical Society of Victoria, South Yarra
The Astronomical Society of South Australia, The Levels
Canberra Astronomical Society, Woden
The Astronomical Society of WA, Subiaco
The Astronomical Society of Alice Springs, Alice Springs
The Astronomical Society of NSW
Brisbane Astronomical Society, Kelvin Grove

Canada
Royal Astronomical Society of Canada, 136, Dupont St, Toronto, ON M5R IV2

Assoc. des Groupes d'Astronomes Amateurs, 4545, Ave. Pierre-de-Coubertin, Casier postal 1000, Succursale M, Montreal, QC H1V 3RZ

Great Britain
British Astronomical Association, Burlington House, Piccadilly, London W1V 9AG
Federation of Astronomical Societies, C/O Christine Sheldon, Whitehaven, Maytree Road, Lower Moor, Pershore, Worcs. WR10 2NY

New Zealand
Royal Astronomical Society of New Zealand, P.O. Box 318, Wellington
Dunedin Astronomical Society, P.O. Box 8019, Dunedin
Astronautics Assoc. of NZ, Inc. (a spaceflight awareness assoc.), P.O. Box 11-734, Wellington, NZ

United States of America
Amateur Astronomers Assoc., 1010, Park Ave., New York, NY 10028

Answers

Page 6. 30AU.

Divide 4,496,000,000 by 149,600,000 (or 2,793,500,000 by 92,957,000). You could leave the last three 0s off the end of both figures to calculate.

Page 8. You would be 12.

9 Mercurian years = 792 Earth days.
792 ÷ 365 (days in an Earth year) = 2.16
10 years + 2.16 = 12.16

Page 24. 14,199. It's easiest to work it all out in hours:

248 Earth years is 248 x 365 (days in a year) x 24(hours in a day) = 2,172,480
6 days 9 hours = 6 x 24 + 9 = 153
2,172,480 ÷ 153 = 14,199.22

The history of astronomy

Astronomy is the oldest of all the sciences. Ever since the first people appeared on Earth they have been curious about what they can see in the sky.

The first stargazers

We know cavemen watched the night sky because they drew what they saw on their cave walls. People realized that the heavens were useful when they found that watching the movements of the Sun, Moon and stars could help them plan the best times to plant and harvest their crops.

This shows the prehistoric monument, Stonehenge, in Wiltshire, England.

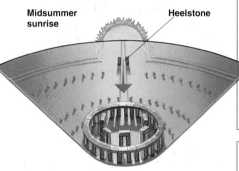

Midsummer sunrise

Heelstone

Stonehenge may have been erected to mark the position of the rising midsummer Sun.

Chinese star maps

The Ancient Chinese studied the night sky and drew it on stone and parchment, recording any changes they witnessed. These were the first sky maps.

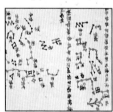

Ancient Chinese map of the heavens

Birth of true astronomy

Ancient Egyptians used the Moon, Sun and stars to plan their festivals and events; but it was the Ancient Greeks who turned looking at the sky into a science. One of them, Hipparchus, drew a very accurate map of the night sky.

Ptolemy

It was not until 150 AD that the first patterns of stars - or constellations - were set down. Ptolemy listed 48 of them in his book *The Almagest*. This book gave a structure for the Universe based on the work of the earlier Greek philosopher, Aristotle (384-322 BC). Ptolemy said Earth was at the hub of everything, orbited by the Sun, Moon and planets. He thought the stars were points of light set on the inside of a revolving sphere. This sphere surrounded Earth and all things moving around Earth.

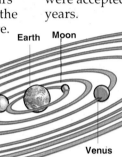

An old map of the Ptolemaic System

Ptolemy also thought the sky could never change. His ideas were accepted as true for 1400 years.

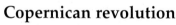

Saturn

Mars

Earth Moon Sun Jupiter

Mercury

Venus

This is what the Ptolemaic system, with the Earth central, looked like.

Copernican revolution

In 1543, Ptolemy's ideas were challenged by a Polish monk, Mikolaj Kopernigk, now known by his Latin name, Copernicus. His Heliocentric theory (Helios was the Ancient Greek god of the Sun) placed the Sun as the focus of the Universe, not the Earth. The Church, which had supported Ptolemy for many years because his theory agreed with the Bible, was so angry with Copernicus that he was too frightened to publish his ideas. When Copernicus finally did publish *De Revolutionibus Orbium Coelestium*

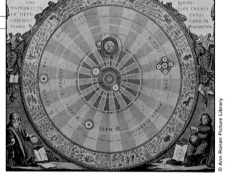

An old map of the Copernican system

(*On the Revolution of the Heavenly Spheres*) it prompted much debate and speculation about the true nature of the Universe.

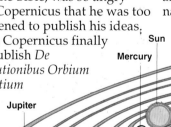

Sun Venus Earth Mars Saturn

Mercury

Jupiter

Moon

Copernicus's system looks much like today's Solar System.

Tycho Brahe

One astronomer who took up the challenge was the Dane, Tycho Brahe. His detailed observations of a brilliant, exploding star - now known as a supernova - in 1572, and a comet several years later, convinced him that Copernicus was right: the sky could change.

This is Tycho Brahe's observatory in Denmark.

This put Brahe in a dilemma. He knew Ptolemy was wrong, but because he was a very religious man and loyal to the Church he could not accept Copernicus's theory either.

A champion for Copernicus

Brahe carried on with his studies and when he died Johannes Kepler, his German assistant, continued his work, under instructions to disprove Copernicus's theories once and for all. Loyal Kepler tried very hard to fulfil Brahe's wishes, but everything he saw convinced him that Copernicus was right: the planets orbited the Sun, but in oval paths, not circles as Copernicus had predicted.

Copernicus's circling orbits.

Kepler's oval orbits.

Long before gravity was discovered, Kepler suggested that the Sun influenced how the planets moved. There was little interest in his idea at the time, but it revolutionized astronomy after his death.

Invention of the telescope

Although astronomers had begun to build up a picture of the nature and structure of the Universe, it took the invention of the telescope to let them see things in detail. In 1608, Hans Lippershey (see page 32) found that if a pair of lenses was lined up it magnified distant objects. To make the lenses easier to use he mounted them at opposite ends of a long tube, making the first telescope.

Here, two of Lippershey's apprentices test his discovery.

Galileo's observations

Word of Lippershey's invention spread quickly and astronomers realized its potential. In 1609 Galileo (also see page 32) built improved versions, which he pointed at the sky.

What he saw amazed him. The Moon had mountains and craters; spots moved across the Sun's face; Jupiter had tiny moons, and Venus changed its shape as time passed.

This last discovery was the most important of all. The way Venus changed shape proved it orbited the Sun and not Earth. At last scientific observations proved Copernicus was right.

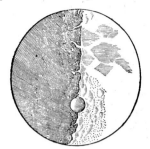

Galileo's sketches of the Moon showed amazing detail.

Punished for the truth

Galileo's observations were very important, but once more the Church supported Ptolemy's old ideas and declared Galileo guilty of blasphemy (irreverence toward God). He was threatened with torture and, in the end, had to deny his work.

Amazing discoveries

With the aid of telescopes, astronomy advanced in great leaps. In 1631, Gassendi saw Mercury move across the Sun. A detailed map of the Moon was published in 1647 by Hevelius. In 1659, Huygens saw the first markings on Mars. Cassini discovered its polar caps in 1666.

A beautiful stand held Galileo's long, thin telescope tubes.

Newton

The English physicist and astronomer Isaac Newton wrote a book called *The Principia* in 1687, which changed the way we view the Universe and our place in it forever. It contained his ideas about gravity (see page 4). It is often said that Newton discovered gravity when he saw an apple drop from a tree. That told him there was a force of attraction between the Earth and other objects which pulls them down. Newton's calculations proved Kepler was right and Ptolemy was wrong, and showed that the Universe was stable and was ruled and shaped by gravity.

Because of this, astronomers were suddenly able to predict with great accuracy where objects had been in the past, and would be in the future. This was a huge advance for astronomy.

A new planet is found

On 13th March 1781, English astronomer, William Herschel discovered a new planet beyond Saturn. Using a home-made telescope he observed what he thought was a comet, but further observations and calculations proved it was a planet twice as far from the Sun as Saturn. In one stroke Herschel had doubled the size of the Solar System. The new planet was named Uranus after the father of Saturn. Soon, observations revealed that Uranus was not where it should have been. Something was pulling at it from beyond.

Herschel's home-made telescope

An asteroid discovered

Astronomers started to hunt for planets beyond Uranus, but they found much smaller objects they called asteroids instead. The first, Ceres, was found in 1801 by Italian, Giuseppi Piazzi.

The discovery of Neptune

By 1845, Britain's John Couch Adams had calculated a possible position for a planet beyond Uranus. Frenchman Urbain Jean Leverrier had also calculated one and in 1846 he wrote to the German astronomer Galle and asked him to look for it with his telescope. Galle found it almost at once; but although Galle was first to see the new planet, its discovery was credited to Leverrier and Adams. It was named Neptune, after the Ancient Roman god of the sea.

Neptune

Edwin Hubble

During the 1930s, Edwin Hubble proved that a patch of light in the sky was another galaxy far beyond our own. This suggested that other such clouds were also galaxies, and the size of the known Universe grew millions of times. One year later he proved that the whole Universe was expanding.

This is a galaxy called Andromeda.

The discovery of Pluto

In 1930, after photographing the sky for many years, astronomer Clyde Tombaugh found a ninth planet, named Pluto after the Ancient Greek god of the Underworld.

The Big Bang theory

In 1965, two radio astronomers, Arno Penzias and Robert Wilson, found evidence that the Universe formed in a huge explosion (the Big Bang), supporting a theory which had been popular for many years (see pages 30-31).

Astronomy in space

After being hindered for centuries by Earth's shifting and polluted atmosphere, in the late 1960s astronomers began to place telescopes and instruments in rockets. They could then observe the Universe from orbit, and enjoy a much better view. Astronomers also sent out robot spaceprobes like the Voyagers to explore the Solar System. They took amazing pictures of the planets and their moons. In 1990, the Hubble Space Telescope (named after Edwin Hubble) was placed in orbit. Since then it has made many incredible discoveries.

Luna 9 probe

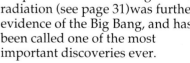

Pioneer Venus 2 probe

Ripples from the Big Bang

The COBE satellite's 1992 discovery of "ripples" - tiny variations in temperature - in the background radiation (see page 31)was further evidence of the Big Bang, and has been called one of the most important discoveries ever.

COBE

The future of astronomy

There are many exciting projects which may revolutionize the science of astronomy over the next few decades.

Bigger, better telescopes

The new generation of telescopes will use much larger mirrors, which will reveal much fainter objects than ever before, and "adaptive optics" will allow astronomers to change slightly the shape of the mirrors to reduce the distorting effect of the atmosphere. The international Gemini telescope will consist of a pair of identical reflectors, one in South America, the other in Hawaii, working together.

This is what one of the Gemini reflecting telescopes will look like.

Spaceprobes

Voyager 2's 1989 encounter with Neptune ended the "First Phase" of planetary exploration. A new fleet of much more sophisticated probes is now spreading out through the Solar System to start Phase 2. The Galileo probe (see page 18) will soon be sending back many thousands of new photographs. The Russians plan to drop balloons onto Mars within the next 10 years.

A Mars balloon will look like this.

Instrument package, including cameras.

The balloons will drag instruments along the ground as they are blown along by the wind. There are also plans to send spaceprobes to map Venus and Mercury in detail, and to study comets from close range. A probe may even try to land on a comet nucleus and return a piece of it to Earth. Missions to photograph and take samples of asteroids are also planned. The Cassini probe will show us Saturn in more detail than ever before and drop a probe into the murky atmosphere of its moon, Titan. Astronomers are also keen to send a probe to study tiny, distant Pluto. Pluto is so small and far away that even the most powerful telescopes on, or above, Earth don't show it as more than a dot of light. A probe might show craters, polar caps and seas of frozen methane gas. Its lone moon, Charon, may also be photographed.

Astronomy on the Moon

When astronauts return to the Moon, early in the next century it is hoped, it is likely that they will start to build large radio and optical telescopes there.

With so little gravity on the Moon, telescopes could be enormous.

With no wind, atmosphere or weather, artificial lights or radio interference, the Moon would make an ideal location for an observatory. The lack of gravity means very large, heavy mirrors could be used there, too.

Potential discoveries?

While amateurs are hoping that a bright comet or supernova will appear soon, professionals are hoping to discover many more "planetesimals" (very small bodies), proving that the Kuiper Belt (page 25) exists. They also hope to find active volcanoes on Venus, evidence of underground water deposits on Mars or even signs of life on the planet. The greatest discovery of all would be the detection of signals sent from another civilization out in space. SETI (Search for Extra-Terrestrial Intelligence) is not science fiction. Even though many astronomers doubt such signals will ever be detected, others

This is Arecibo's (see page 33) coded message.

are convinced mankind is just one of many races in our Galaxy and are carrying out detailed and ambitious searches for alien signals. If any are ever detected, it could be the most important discovery in the history of the human race. We would finally know that we are not alone in the Universe.

Star maps - April-June

On the next eight pages are 16 star maps. There are two for each season in the northern and southern hemispheres, one looking north and one looking south. This is because you can see different stars from different places on Earth and the slice of sky you see changes as the Earth orbits the Sun.

To use the maps, choose the right hemisphere and season and look in the direction shown. Dates and times are given since the sky only looks exactly like the maps at these times. Below each map it says which constellations (in capital letters) and stars to look for. The Moon and planets are not shown.

Northern hemisphere

April 1st 10.00pm
May 1st 8.00pm
June 1st 6.00pm

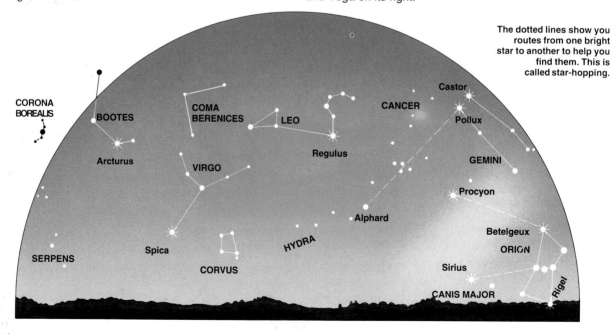

URSA MAJOR

To Leo

To Arcturus

AURIGA
Capella
Polaris
URSA MINOR
DRACO
CORONA BOREALIS
PERSEUS
CASSIOPEIA
CEPHEUS
TAURUS
Algol
Pleiades
Aldebaran
ANDROMEDA
TRIANGULUM
HERCULES
Vega
Deneb
CYGNUS
OPHIUCHUS
Rasalhague

West   **Looking North**   East

Now is a good time to look for the famous Plough of URSA MAJOR, the Great Bear, overhead and TAURUS The Bull setting in the west.

The star Polaris, which never changes its position, is flanked by Capella and Aldebaran on its left, and Deneb and Vega on its right.

The dotted lines show you routes from one bright star to another to help you find them. This is called star-hopping.

CORONA BOREALIS
BOOTES
COMA BERENICES
LEO
CANCER
Castor
Pollux
Arcturus
VIRGO
Regulus
GEMINI
Procyon
Alphard
Betelgeux
ORION
Spica
HYDRA
Sirius
Rigel
SERPENS
CORVUS
CANIS MAJOR

East   **Looking south**   West

LEO, The Lion, dominates the sky, with VIRGO, The Virgin, following ORION, The Hunter, is setting in the west.

Regulus shines in the centre of the sky, with Arcturus and Spica to its left and several bright winter stars on its right.

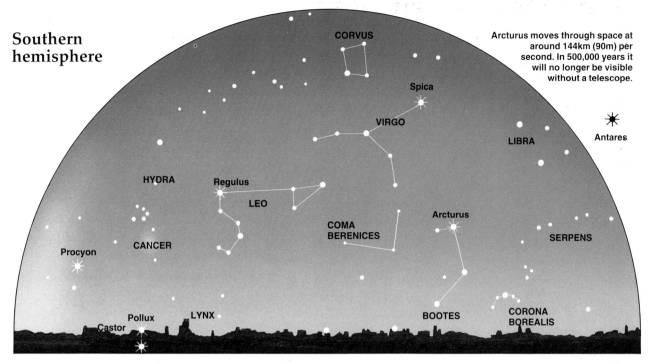

Southern hemisphere

CORVUS

Spica

VIRGO

LIBRA

Antares

HYDRA

Regulus

LEO

COMA BERENICES

Arcturus

SERPENS

CANCER

Procyon

BOOTES

CORONA BOREALIS

Pollux

LYNX

Castor

Arcturus moves through space at around 144km (90m) per second. In 500,000 years it will no longer be visible without a telescope.

West   *Looking north*   *East*

Compared to the southern sky in this hemisphere, the northern sky is quite bare, but for LEO The Lion and VIRGO The Virgin.

A triangle of three bright stars dominates the sky looking north: it consists of Regulus, which is blue, yellow Arcturus and blue-white Spica.

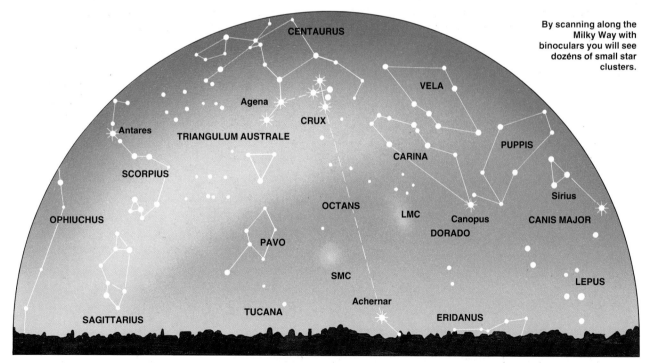

CENTAURUS

VELA

Agena

CRUX

TRIANGULUM AUSTRALE

PUPPIS

Antares

CARINA

SCORPIUS

OCTANS

LMC

Sirius

OPHIUCHUS

Canopus

CANIS MAJOR

DORADO

PAVO

SMC

LEPUS

TUCANA

Achernar

ERIDANUS

SAGITTARIUS

By scanning along the Milky Way with binoculars you will see dozéns of small star clusters.

East   *Looking south*   *West*

Here you can see CRUX, which is known as The Southern Cross, almost overhead. It is enveloped in the Milky Way which crosses the sky in a wide band.

Ruddy red Antares is high in the east and Canopus is lower down to the west. Just above the southern horizon is Achernar.

July-September

Northern hemisphere

In summer, the sky never gets truly dark and only the brightest stars can be seen properly.

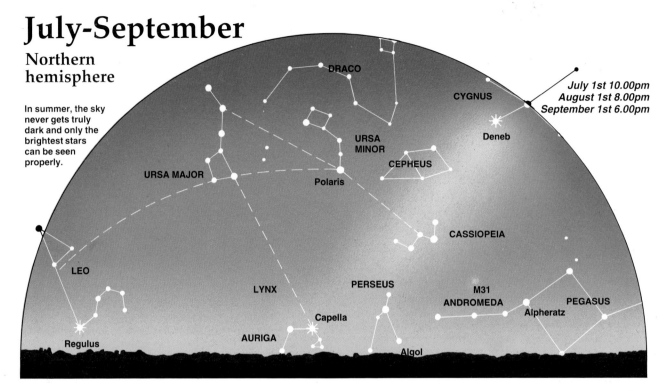

July 1st 10.00pm
August 1st 8.00pm
September 1st 6.00pm

West · **Looking north** · *East*

URSA MAJOR is now dropping down nearer to the northern horizon, as is LEO. PEGASUS and ANDROMEDA are rising in the east.

The bright yellow star called Capella hangs just above the horizon, with Regulus off to its left and bright Deneb high up in the east.

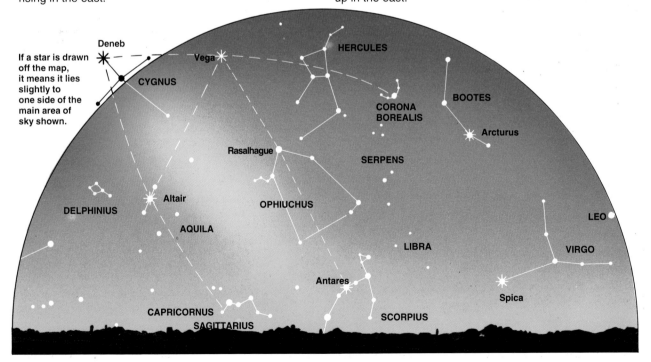

If a star is drawn off the map, it means it lies slightly to one side of the main area of sky shown.

East · **Looking south** · *West*

The bright middle part of the Milky Way can be seen above the southern horizon, with the Scorpion of SCORPIUS shining within it.

Ruddy Antares shines brightly just above the summer southern horizon; brilliant blue Vega is almost overhead and close to Deneb.

Southern hemisphere

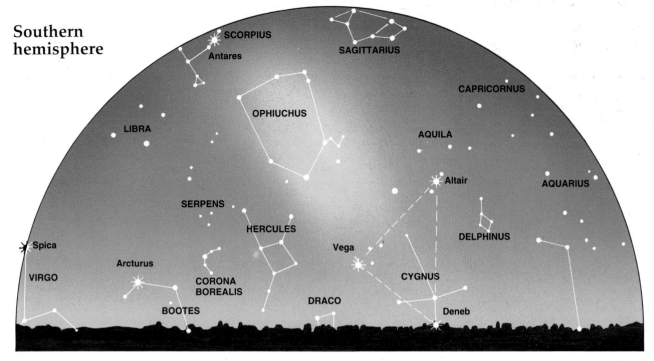

West   **Looking north**   **East**

The Milky Way is seen at its best here, cutting the sky in half. SAGITTARIUS The Archer is overhead, CYGNUS The Swan lower.

The northern sky is dominated by the summer triangle of Vega, Deneb and Altair. Ruby red Antares also shines almost overhead.

To find due south, join the second brightest of the two pointer stars to the Southern Cross to Achernar. The midpoint of this line is due south.

Antares is a red giant star. It has a diameter of 960 million km (597 million mi).

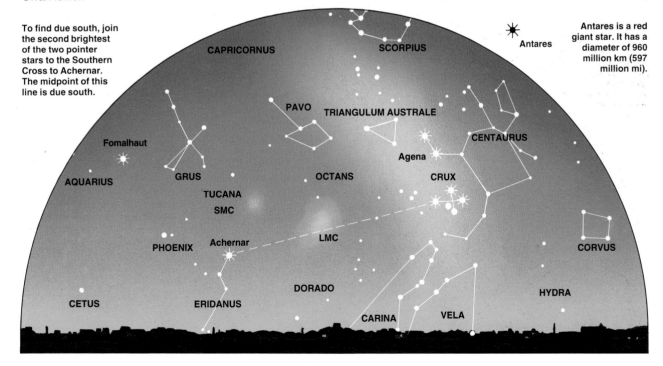

Looking south   **West**

The skies of the southern hemisphere are full of bright stars in late winter and early spring: Deneb, Arcturus, Spica, Altair, Vega and Fomalhaut all shine like jewels.

October - December

Northern hemisphere

October 1st 10.00pm
November 1st 8.00pm
December 1st 6.00pm

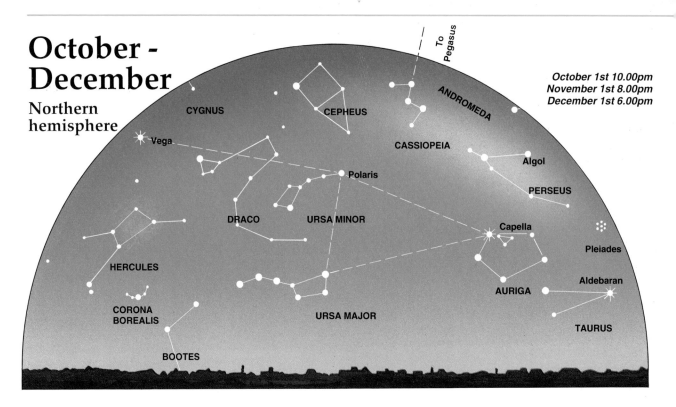

West   **Looking north**   *East*

The Plough of URSA MAJOR is now to be found beneath Polaris and parallel to the horizon. To its right lies AURIGA, The Charioteer.

In the east the winter stars are beginning to rise , including the ruddy red star Aldebaran. The Pleiades cluster comes trailing behind.

This is the best time of year to see M31, a huge galaxy more than 2 million light years beyond our own. It is just visible to the naked eye, but is best seen through binoculars.

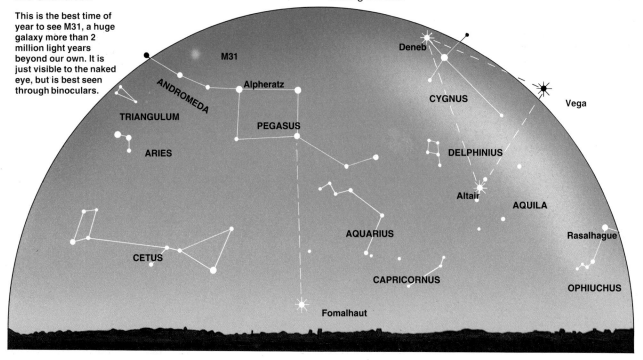

East   **Looking south**   *West*

The autumn sky is dominated by PEGASUS The Winged Horse and ANDROMEDA The Maiden. CYGNUS lies to the west in the Milky Way.

To the east, the summer triangle of Altair, Deneb and Vega shines brightly, while Fomalhaut flashes just above the horizon.

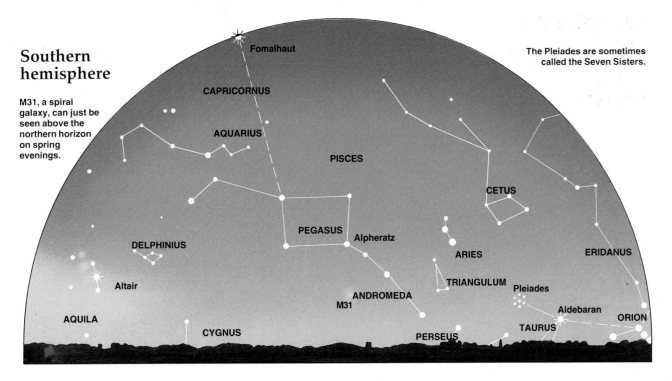

Southern hemisphere

M31, a spiral galaxy, can just be seen above the northern horizon on spring evenings.

The Pleiades are sometimes called the Seven Sisters.

Fomalhaut

CAPRICORNUS

AQUARIUS

PISCES

CETUS

PEGASUS

Alpheratz

ARIES

ERIDANUS

DELPHINIUS

TRIANGULUM

Pleiades

Altair

ANDROMEDA

M31

Aldebaran

ORION

AQUILA

TAURUS

CYGNUS

PERSEUS

West

Looking north

East

PEGASUS and ANDROMEDA dominate the northern sky. In the east ORION The Hunter is rising. AQUILA The Eagle lies to the west.

While blue Altair flashes in the west, white Fomalhaut shines brightly overhead and ruby red Aldebaran blazes in the east.

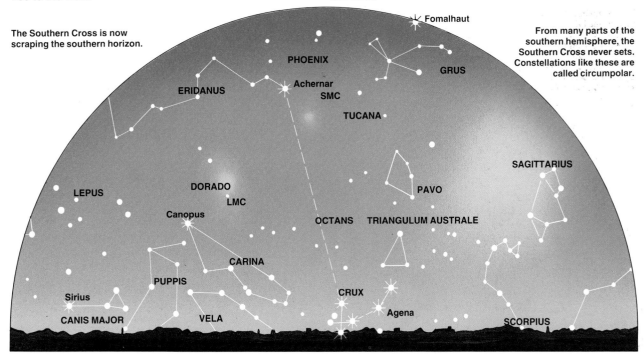

The Southern Cross is now scraping the southern horizon.

From many parts of the southern hemisphere, the Southern Cross never sets. Constellations like these are called circumpolar.

Fomalhaut

PHOENIX

GRUS

ERIDANUS

Achernar

SMC

TUCANA

SAGITTARIUS

LEPUS

DORADO

LMC

PAVO

Canopus

OCTANS

TRIANGULUM AUSTRALE

CARINA

PUPPIS

Sirius

CRUX

Agena

CANIS MAJOR

VELA

SCORPIUS

East

Looking south

West

The misty Milky Way lies parallel to the horizon now. The SOUTHERN CROSS is very low, and PHOENIX The Phoenix is overhead.

Canopus, the second brightest of all the stars, shines to the east of diamond-like Sirius, which is the brightest star in the sky.

45

January - March

Northern hemisphere

As Autumn's stars sink into the west, bright blue Deneb can just be seen above the northern horizon from northern latitudes.

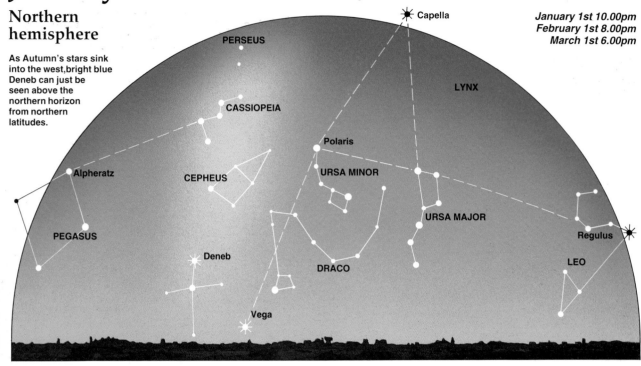

January 1st 10.00pm
February 1st 8.00pm
March 1st 6.00pm

West   **Looking north**   *East*

As the year ends URSA MAJOR, the Great Bear, balances on its tail and CYGNUS dives towards the west, Spring constellation LEO rises in the east.

Bright yellow Capella shines directly overhead as blue Deneb and Vega drop towards the west. Blue Regulus is flashing in the east.

Winter is another good time for shooting stars, as the Geminid meteor shower lights up the sky in mid-December.

Orion will help guide you to many of the winter sky's constellations and star clusters.

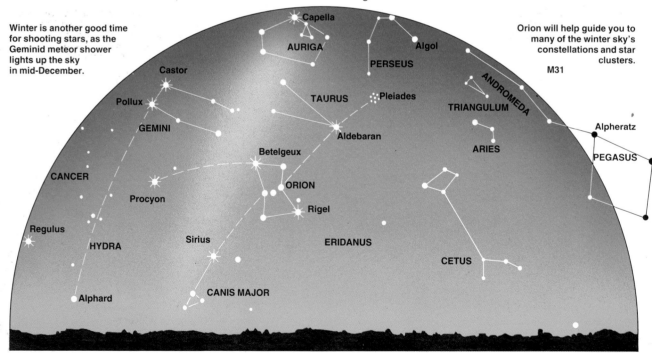

East   **Looking south**   *West*

ORION The Hunter dominates the southern sky, with CANIS MAJOR The Great Dog, TAURUS The Bull and GEMINI The Twins.

The sky is full of beautiful, bright and varied stars. Look out for red Betelgeuse and Aldebaran, Rigel which is blue, and white Sirius.

Southern hemisphere

Over to the east you can see the Sickle of LEO looking like a fish hook.

The middle star of the three in a row in ORION looks like a misty patch in binoculars. It is where a star is being born.

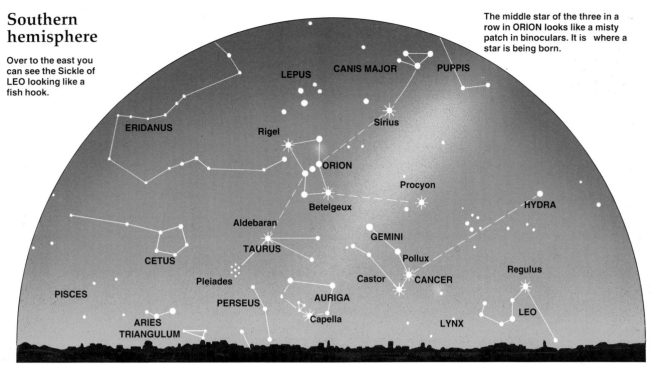

West   **Looking north**   *East*

Impressive ORION, The Hunter, rules the sky surrounded by TAURUS The Bull, GEMINI The Twins, and CANIS MAJOR and CANIS MINOR.

The northern sky in winter looks as if it has been scattered with jewels: Betelgeuse, Rigel, Castor and Pollux all blaze gloriously.

Alpha Centauri is the nearest star to us, after the Sun. It is 4.3 light years away. That's 274,000 times further than our Sun.

LMC and SMC stand for Large and Small Magellanic Cloud. These are small, satellite galaxies of the Milky Way which look like faint, misty patches of light.

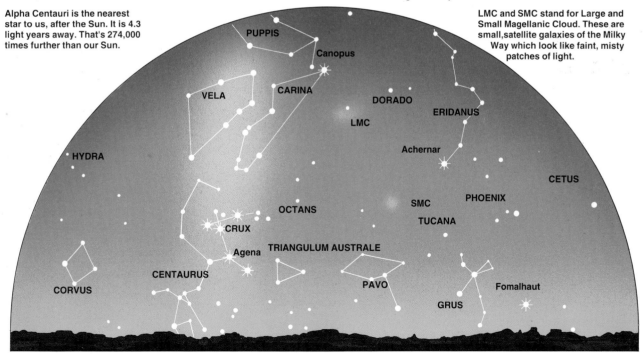

East   **Looking south**   *West*

The southern sky is dominated by CENTAURUS, The Centaur, which wraps around CRUX. VELA, The Sail, and CARINA, The Keel, lie above.

There are few bright stars in the southern sky at this time. Canopus shines close to overhead, while Achernar and Fomalhaut lie to the east.

Index